I0591631

BLUE EYES AND OTHER TALES

GRYPHON INSURRECTION STORIES

K. VALE NAGLE

STET PUBLISHING, LLC

Cover Art by Fleeks Sputtelspecht (www.fleeks.art).

Interior graphics by Crystal Gafford of Crafty as a Coyote.

Published by STET Publishing, Denver

WWW.STETPUBLISHING.COM

WWW.KVALENAGLE.COM

Trade Paperback Edition
ISBN: 1-64392-029-4
ISBN-13: 978-1-64392-029-0

To all of my fans who sent me email, supported me on Patreon, replied to my newsletter, volunteered to be beta readers, or just told another living soul about my books. I wrote these stories to say thank you.

BLUE EYES

"**B**ut the aneda forest is cold!" Satra whined. Her adult feathers felt bulky, her paws were too big, and she didn't want to have to go all the way across the nesting grounds just to hunt every day.

Thenca sighed. "You're not a gryphlet anymore, little flamecrest. You're not even a fledgling. You have to earn your place. Otherwise, they'll cast you out, and you'll have to go live with the fisherfolk."

Satra countered Thenca's sigh with her own exasperated exhalation. "Fisherfolk aren't real. You made me fly down to the mangroves, remember? There were no gryphons there, just crabs and manatees."

Thenca massaged her head the way she did whenever Satra was acting unreasonable. "The aneda forests aren't so bad. I hunt in the ones north of the river. They can be a lot of fun."

Satra wasn't convinced. "They're easy for you because you have big wings and a bushy tail, so you can stay warm."

Thenca flapped her wings loudly and made a bird sound to make Satra laugh. "Come along. I'll use my giant thunderbird wings to fly down with you and help you get started. Then I'll pick you up when it's time to come home. Sound good?"

Satra managed one last sigh, then a laugh. "Okay, let's do it!"

DESPITE THENCA'S promise of fun, Satra was soon cold, wet, and hungry. Her only consolation was that the black flies were leaving her alone. Unfortunately, so were the swamp grouse, frogs, and everything else big enough for her to eat.

She sat down along the edge of a large, frozen lake and began to push snow into a pile with her paws. Someday, she'd be a great hunter. Not just a great hunter, she'd be the best hunter—and flyer, too. Today, however, she was Jun the Kjarr's daughter, and they weren't going to let her go hungry if she came back empty-beaked.

She started compacting the snow into a snow-gryphon. She got the outline right, but it was hard to make feathers with snow, so she went to fetch some aneda branches for the wings. She peeled off some bark for the beak and was feeling pretty good about her first snow-gryphon efforts when she accidentally stepped on the tail.

"Oh, well, I guess you can be Urious and not Thenca," she said to her masterpiece.

Satra had just finished finding two seed cones for the eyes when she heard a *ribbit* behind her. She dropped down low and stalked to the edge of the frozen lake. Twenty feet away, a frog the size of her face hopped across the ice.

She didn't know why this particular frog had defrosted so early into the season, but it was big enough to eat. Sure, her sister would laugh at Satra if she only came back with a frog, but Vitra was always looking for reasons to pick on her younger sibling. It would be a lot easier to endure the teasing with a full stomach.

Satra tried her best to stay calm, but her tail twitched back and forth at the thought of eating such a large frog. Just when she was certain the shaking would catch the attention of her prey, she leapt onto the ice.

Her pounce caught the frog, but she forgot to extend her claws, and it slipped through her paws and hopped away. Meanwhile, Satra was slipping and spinning. She didn't seem to be slowing at all, and she let out a yowl.

When her scrabbling claws finally stopped her spin, she was fifty feet from the shore. She was grateful she hadn't caught anything to eat this morning because she'd have thrown it up. She carefully lifted herself off her stomach and onto her paws. She pushed off to fly back to shore, but her legs splayed out in all directions, and she fell on her face.

From the shore, she heard someone giggle.

"Who's there?" Satra squeaked. "I am Satra, Daughter of the Kjarr, and I won't be laughed at!"

The snowbank seemed to crawl onto the ice. Satra wiped at her eyes, then realized it wasn't snow, it was a taiga gryphon. The bright blue eyes gave her away.

The stranger walked across the frozen lake as though it were solid rock, and for a moment, Satra thought she might be seeing a bog witch.

But no, this was definitely a taiga gryphon. She wandered right up to Satra and touched the tip of Satra's beak with her paw. "Hello there, Satra, Daughter of the Kjarr. You seem to have a bit of a problem."

"Who are you?" Satra demanded. She'd never met a taiga gryphon before. She'd never met *any* gryphon outside of her pride before except for the bog gryphons, and they didn't count.

"Mignet of Snowfall," the stranger said with a bow and spread wings. Her front half resembled a gyrfalcon, all white with black bars, and her back half had thick white fur and pretty black rosettes. She had on a sea-leather harness and a silver bracelet. No kjarr gryphons wore harnesses or jewelry, though some of the bog gryphons used feather paint.

Satra tried to stand up and return the bow but ended up falling back on her stomach, eliciting another giggle from her companion.

"What type of gryphon are you?" Mignet extended a claw and used it to pull up Satra's crest. She put her face right up next to the golden feathers and peered at them. The rest of Satra's plumage, unlike Mignet's, was a mixture of dull browns and greys.

Satra managed to get herself back in a standing position. It required four paws and her tail on the ground. "I'm a kjarr gryphon. Hence, being daughter of the Kjarr."

"Oh, well then," the stranger said. "Then I guess I'm Mignet, Daughter of the Snowfall."

Satra wasn't sure if Mignet was teasing her or if her father was the taiga pride leader. Satra had heard Urious talk about him in the past: he was one of the three plague-born, gryphons who had survived the monitor plague that had killed every other child of their hatch year. It was said they had a special immunity to the affliction.

"No, 'kjarr' is a place and a title," Satra tried to explain. "The kjarr is the aneda forests and river here. But it's also the name of my father, Jun the Kjarr, who rules it."

Mignet walked around to Satra's back and was poking her tail to see if it made her fall. "Sounds complicated. Why not just say pride leader?"

"Because the leader of the kjarr pride makes a promise to—" Satra began, but Mignet gave her a push, and she was back to sliding towards shore.

Satra stiffened her legs and tail and managed not to fall this time, though she was afraid to start walking.

Mignet flew over and landed next to her. "Well, we're a little closer. We'll figure this out, Daughter of the Kjarr, and get you back home in no time."

Satra bristled. "This is my home. Wherever there are aneda forests is kjarr pride territory."

Mignet laughed. "Wherever there are mountains is taiga territory."

They both looked around. They were in the mountains but at a low enough altitude that the aneda trees were still growing.

"I guess it's both of ours?" Satra offered. She didn't want to offend her only hope at getting back to solid ground. She had visions of Thenca coming to the frozen lake and finding Satra still stuck here.

Mignet circled around behind Satra, reared up on her back legs to look as tall as possible. Her wings flared in a halo behind her, and she adopted a storyteller's tone. "We shall rule it together, the Daughters of the Kjarr and Snowfall!"

Then she placed her front paws on Satra's hindquarters, and in addition to running behind her with her back paws, which somehow had traction, she beat her wings to build speed. Satra began to slide, and Mignet steered her. They were nearly to the shore when suddenly Mignet turned them back towards the center of the lake and gained momentum.

"What are you doing?!" Satra cried.

"Having fun!" Mignet shouted back. "Here, put your

wings out. It'll be just like flying."

Mignet hopped on top of Satra and wrapped her front paws around the kjarr gryphon. They were moving pretty fast now, but Mignet shouted at Satra to open her right wing, and they turned back towards shore.

Just when things slowed down, Mignet put her back paws on the ground and started pushing again to build up momentum. "To the far shore! We shall be fisherfolk together, conquering the frozen seas!"

Satra used her wings to turn them back towards the ice, closed her eyes, decided that just made it worse, and opened them again. This time, Mignet held their wings closed, and the speed didn't let up.

"How are you steering?" Satra shouted.

"Tailfeathers!" Mignet's feathered tail, a rarity for a gryphon, shifted back and forth, keeping them on course.

"We're going too fast!" Satra tried to open her wings to slow down, but Mignet's wings kept hers pinned against her body.

"We've got this," Mignet said. "Hold steady, Fisherfolk Satra, and trust the tailfeathers."

As the far shore loomed closer and closer, Satra began to panic. She tried to crouch down to slow herself, but that just put her passenger off balance. Soon, they were both tumbling and sliding. It turned out that while Mignet's paws were good at holding traction, the rest of her was as slippery as Satra.

"Aaaaah!" Satra shouted as she hit the shore.

"Ahahaha!" Mignet echoed as she crashed after Satra.

Snow cushioned their impact and went flying into the air. They pulled themselves out of the snowbank and up to a rocky outcropping that was soaking up the sun's warmth to preen themselves dry.

Once the thrill had passed, Satra sighed. "I almost had that frog."

"I didn't see any frog. I just saw you pouncing the ice," Mignet said. She shook her wings out separately, then her tailfeathers.

"It was there!" Satra protested. "It was a big one, the size of my head."

"That's pretty big," Mignet admitted. "Both your head and your imaginary frog."

She leaned in to look at the size of Satra's head. Their beaks were close enough to touch, and all Satra could see were Mignet's blue eyes.

"It was a real frog," Satra protested. "And you're going to help me catch it! You can be my paws on the ice. I'll chase it back onto the lake, and you grab it, and we'll split it for lunch."

"I think you're crazy," Mignet said. "Sure, the weather has been heating up, but frogs don't defrost until the snow melts. But you're cute, so I'll humor you. You are a guest in my home, after all."

Satra took a paw and ruffled the taiga gryphon's head feathers. "I think you mean that you're a guest in my home."

"Guests and hosts," Mignet chirped, "both need lunch. Let's find your hopper."

It took some searching, but Satra was vindicated when she located the frog. With Mignet's steady-footed help, they managed to catch it.

"They're sweeter if you eat them while they're frozen," Mignet said between bites of her half. "It's too bad there are no breaks in the lake. One dunk in the water and it'd refreeze. At least, that works for sugar frogs. I think this might be a lost bog hopper."

"Hopper, Daughter of the Bog," Satra teased, but Mignet was listening to the cry of a snowy owl in the distance.

"That's Deracho, letting me know that my father needs me back at Snowfall," Mignet apologized. If she'd said the den mother or den father had wanted her back, it would have been different, but the way she phrased things made Satra certain her father must be the plagueborn pride leader. "I've had fun. This is my hunting territory. If you're around tonight, I'll be back. If not, maybe I'll run into you tomorrow."

She pushed her paw against Satra's face, then got a running start and took to the air, slowly climbing the mountains to return home. Thenca arrived only moments later, startling Satra out of her daydreaming.

"Hey, you caught a frog. Good job!" Thenca said.

"Oh, yes, I did," Satra stammered. "It's not enough to bring home to the pride, but it was enough to feed myself."

Thenca's brow furrowed. "Your nares are bright red. Are you catching cold? Are you sick? Let's get you back to the kjarr so you can warm up."

Satra assured Thenca that she was fine but didn't admit she'd been thinking about a pretty taiga gryphon.

They got back to the kjarr nesting grounds, and Satra went to find her father to ask him about the taiga pride. He was busy hunting with Vitra and her brother, so Satra wandered back to the main nests to sleep. They were full of loud gryphlets and grumpy fledglings, and she slipped away to Thenca's home, nestled along the bank of the river, just far back enough to stay dry.

"Can I stay with you tonight?" Satra asked.

Thenca was preening her feathers to perfection. "I'm afraid I have some night hunting to do."

Satra didn't know night hunting was a thing and said so.

"It isn't, usually," Thenca admitted. "And you shouldn't go out at night on your own. It can be dangerous. But I've noticed the swamp grouse are more active after dark, so I've been experimenting."

Satra shrugged. "Well, can I stay in your nest until you get back?"

Thenca started to say no but caught herself. "Satra, you need to stop procrastinating and build your own nest. But yes, you can stay here just for tonight. You're going to have to go out hunting on your own tomorrow, though. Can you do that?"

Satra flopped down on Thenca's nest and pretended to snore.

"This is why I could never be a den mother." Thenca finished her grooming and slipped out into the night, leaving Satra to quit her fake snoring and actually fall asleep.

SATRA MANAGED to borrow Thenca's nest for two more weeks before she was finally cast out. She'd fallen asleep with a squirrel she'd meant to eat later. It turned out the squirrel was in shock and not dead, so while Satra slept, it burrowed into the nest. When Thenca got back from her night hunting to sleep, the squirrel woke up and went berserk.

Satra ran off to go hunting as Thenca shouted after her, escaping into the safety of the aneda forest. Now far from Thenca's wrath, Satra gathered aneda branches and put them in a circle. Then she hopped on top, causing them to snap and crunch under her weight.

"What do you think?" she asked.

Mignet stood on the edge of the nest and looked at its

construction, her face nearly touching the branches. She put a paw on the nest and pushed down, testing it. It cracked and gave way. When she pulled her paw back, it was covered in aneda resin. "Looks sticky."

"What?" Satra asked, but when she tried to stand up, most of the nest was sticking to her. She shook out her paws and tail, but the resin held fast. "This is worse than getting shocked on the tail by a knife fish."

"Knife fish?" Mignet asked. She got to work pulling branches out of Satra's feathers and fur. It took a liberal amount of saliva to get the resin out.

"They're long, eel-like fish," Satra explained. "They live in the water, and if you get close, they leap out and shock you. Like static electricity. Zap!"

Mignet laughed. "Sounds exciting in the bog. Or is that the kjarr?"

Satra rolled her eyes. Mignet often teased her about how she used both interchangeably. "Unless you're in the deep bog, it's basically the same, except we have more trees."

"Well, you'll have to show me one of these days," Mignet said. She'd finished getting the resin out of Satra's fur and was trying to clean it from her paw. "I want to see one of these bog wisps you talk about."

Satra looked back at the pile of sticks that made up her practice nest. If she didn't figure this out, she'd be sleeping with the gryphlets and fledglings again, and the den mother was even grumpier than Thenca. "How do taiga gryphons build nests? What do you do for yourself?"

"There's a cave system on top of Snowfall," Mignet explained. "We live in the caves. There's a hot springs, too."

Hot springs sounded nice to a sticky Satra. "Yeah, but you don't just live on the stone floor, right? You sleep on something?"

"Well, I..." Mignet's nares were red. "Okay, I don't know how to build a nest, either. My friends did it for me. Mine's falling apart, and I don't know how to repair it. I'm just too embarrassed to admit as much to the other taiga gryphons."

"Maybe we can figure it out by seeing how yours is made," Satra said. "How far away is Snowfall? Can we go take a look?"

"I can't just sneak a kjarr gryphon into Snowfall," Mignet protested. "What would my father think? Besides, I've seen you fly. You're not good enough to get over the mountains. You need to get a lot better before I'd even consider taking you to my nest."

While Satra knew her flying was worse than average, she didn't like having it pointed out. She was about to let Mignet have a piece of her mind when she heard the familiar call of the snowy owl. She spoke up before Mignet could. "You're needed back home. I get it. Go on, get out of here. I'll figure out how to build a nest all by myself."

"I didn't mean to upset you," Mignet began, but Satra had already turned and was pretending to study her past nest efforts. "Oh, come on. I'm apologizing! We can teach you to fly up high if you want to see Snowfall. I'll show you the hot springs."

Satra continued to ignore Mignet. When Mignet's protests went quiet, Satra became curious, and turned around just in time to see Mignet in a hunter's crouch, her tailfeathers wagging back and forth.

"Mignet, what are you—" was as far as Satra got before Mignet pounced her into the pile of branches. Satra wanted to be mad, but she ended up laughing instead. "Okay, okay! Now help me get unsticky."

Mignet licked Satra's beak and danced away. "Nope, you

can just think of how much you miss me as you pull those twigs out of your fur."

Satra reached out a paw to try to catch Mignet, but she was in the air, heading towards the snowy owl's call. Satra was still grooming branches and resin out of her fur when Thenca showed up, looking tired but happy.

"What's going on here?" Thenca laughed. "Are you trying to build a nest out of fresh aneda branches? That'll never work. You're just going to wake up stuck to the nest!"

"Well, I know that *now*," Satra groused.

Thenca's face lost a little of its happiness. "Did your father not come to show you how to put together a nest? He taught Vitra and your brother."

Satra did her best to keep her voice steady when she said no. Her father had taken an interest in all of her older siblings, but it felt like he'd grown tired of children by the time Satra hatched. Jun was much older than Mignet's father, and in between Vitra and Satra, he'd had one more child who had been lost to the plague. While Urious explained that he was just hesitant to get too attached now, Satra wasn't so sure. She'd met with her father a few times, but he was usually off leading hunting expeditions with her older siblings. Sometimes, she wasn't even sure he knew her name.

Thenca looked up at the light. "We have a little time. Come on, flamecrest, let's head deeper into the bog. I'll help you build a nest that won't stick to you."

THE NEXT DAY, Satra waited for Mignet on the edge of the frozen lake. She'd been practicing standing on ice. While she wasn't graceful and couldn't get into the air like this, she was at least confident she could navigate her way to the shoreline in case of an emergency.

Mignet landed and chirped a greeting.

"Follow me!" Satra shouted, and she headed back west into the kjarr. Mignet looked confused but followed.

They flew to the edge of the mountains, then walked the rest of the way in. They didn't go too far. Satra didn't think there'd be a problem with her escorting Mignet around, but some gryphons were territorial about borders, and she didn't want to get her new friend into trouble.

Once they were past the aneda trees, Satra started to gather branches. "So the key is *not* to use aneda or kashow. At least, that's the easy way of doing it."

Mignet nodded and joined in, finding dry sticks to collect. "I do think my nest at home is aneda. At least, it has that bitter smell, like medicine. It isn't sticky, though."

"Thenca says you can soak and then dry aneda to get the resin out," Satra explained. "But who wants that smell? We'll make a nest out of cypress for you. That way, you can stand out from the other taiga gryphons. When you bring home a mate, they'll be all like, *Oh, Mignet, you're such a great nestmaker. We should have lots of plague-resistant eggs together.*"

Mignet rolled her eyes. "Okay, now that we've figured out nesting, show me these bog wisps and knife fish."

"*Oh, Mignet, your tailfeathers are so pretty. Won't you keep me warm on these cold mountain nights?*" was as far as Satra got before Mignet swatted her beak playfully.

They went deeper into the bog, and the aneda trees gave further way to several types of cypress. There were no bog wisps, but they did find some fish and caught a few eels. Satra pointed out the difference between an eel and a knife fish, and they took them back to the practice nest to eat.

Satra had to pull Mignet away when she tried to look up close at a baby knife fish so she didn't get shocked.

"This is much easier hunting than the aneda forests," Mignet said. "If I could just catch fish, I don't think I'd ever chase frost chickens. Why aren't you hunting out here?"

Satra finished her eel and snuggled close to Mignet. "I don't know, honestly. I thought it was because I'm so young. This is my first hunting ground. But Thenca's hunting in the aneda forest up north, and she's one of my dad's favorites."

Mignet finished her eel and put a wing over Satra. "Thenca's the one with the black mask, fluffy tail, and pretty wings?"

Satra nodded.

"I think she probably requested that stretch herself," Mignet said. "She sneaks away and spends the nights with Deracho by the waterfall."

Satra blinked. "Wait, what? That can't be right. Thenca's not seeing anyone."

"Sure she is," Mignet said. "I see them all the time at night."

"How do you see them?" Satra asked. "Why do you see them at night?"

"'Cause I sneak away, too!" Mignet said. "I sneak away with Younce and watch the stars at night when I can't sleep.

"You sneak away... with Younce?" Satra couldn't hide the dejection from her voice.

Mignet pushed her beak against Satra's and looked her in the eye. "You're jealous?"

Satra nodded her head slightly.

"Of Younce?" Mignet laughed. "Oh my sweet tailfeathers, he's probably related to me! I'm not sneaking away with him or any other taiga gryphon like Thenca is sneaking away with Deracho. Do *you* sneak away with gryphons from your pride?"

"Hey, don't turn this back on me!" Satra pushed aside her embarrassment. "I don't personally, but yes, often my pridemates do. We were two prides once, and there are a lot of us."

"How much is a lot?" Mignet asked. "There are probably fifty taiga gryphons. We're a big pride. Do you have a hundred?"

Satra thought of how far the kjarr nesting grounds stretched down the river. "No, maybe two thousand?"

"I don't know that word. How much is a thousand?" Mignet tilted her head to the side.

Satra extended a claw and traced the Snowfall glyph in the dirt. "That's fifty gryphons, right?"

Mignet nodded. She'd pulled her wing back so it wasn't over Satra anymore.

Satra drew twenty kjarr glyphs on the ground. "That's a thousand." She drew twenty more. "And that's how many gryphons are in the kjarr pride."

"That's a lot of gryphons." Mignet seemed to be having trouble understanding a pride that large. Overhead, the sound of a flight of kjarr gryphons returning from the hunt filled the skies, ruining the idea they were alone in the bog. "I'd like to go back to the taiga now."

"We need to take apart your nest," Satra said. "I wanted it to be a gift for you, so you can replace the one that's breaking down."

Mignet managed a beaky grin, but it was subdued. She kept watching the sky.

They managed to disassemble the cypress branches, but Satra wasn't sure how they were going to get so many sticks back to the taiga from here and said so.

Mignet had an idea. "Here, help me take off my harness. We can tie it around the sticks, then rest the bundle between our wings and take turns as we walk."

Satra had seen Mignet's harness and bracelet before but hadn't commented on them. She'd never seen a gryphon in a harness and wasn't sure what it was for. She also didn't know how to help Mignet remove it.

"Here, unhook me," Mignet said. She pointed at a latch.

It took Satra a few tries, but she managed to unhook it. "What's it for? Your harness, I mean. Not just wrapping around sticks, right? I've never seen anything like it."

Mignet opened a pocket. Inside were supplies. "Mostly, it's for medicine, bandages, things like that. We don't have any medicine gryphons, so we have to take care of ourselves."

"But how do you make something like that?" Satra asked. The best she could do with her paws was to pick up small rocks and throw them at her sister, usually missing. She helped secure the harness around the bundle of wood so they could start walking back towards the taiga.

"Oh, we don't," Mignet said. "We trade aneda resin to the eyries, and they make them for us. Usually the Redwood Valley Eyrie, but this one was a gift from my mom, so it's a Crackling Sea harness."

Satra's head was swimming a little bit. She'd always been told to stay away from the eyries. Opinici lived there, and opinici didn't like gryphons coming near their farms or homes. It was dangerous. The thought that someone could walk right into their cities as a gryphon and trade things was unimaginable.

"Is the Crackling Sea better than the Redwood Valley?" Satra asked. "Does your mom prefer to fly to the sea to trade?"

"Oh, my mom is an opinicus," Mignet said. She shook her tailfeathers. "Isn't it obvious?"

A plagueborn father and an opinicus mother: Satra wasn't sure what to say, so she didn't say anything. They walked out of the kjarr and arrived back in the taiga just in time to hear Deracho's snowy owl hoot letting Mignet know it was time for her to go back to Snowfall.

"I'll see you tomorrow!" Mignet shouted. It took her a few tries to get airborne with the nesting material, but she pulled it off and gained altitude.

Despite Mignet's promise, it would be several days before they saw each other again.

"I HEAR you've been having some trouble hunting," Jun the Kjarr said to his daughter. His long legs and black-backed ears were all he shared with his youngest. Where only her head had a crest of gold, his fur was a tawny color all the way to his wings.

When she stiffened, he added, "But Thenca assures me you're an excellent hunter, and your flying has improved since you were a fledgling. She says she's seen you practicing at high altitude."

"Yes, Father," Satra said. "I'm doing my best."

"Well, the aneda forests aren't the easiest of hunting territory," Jun said. "Do you know why I gave them to you?"

She shook her head.

"Speak up," he commanded.

"No, pride leader." Satra slunk lower to the ground.

"A lot of gryphons start out hunting in the kjarr," he explained. "They catch fish. They hunt down swamp grouse.

Sometimes, they catch a stray capybara that escapes the ranch. It's a pretty easy life."

She nodded, then added, "Yes, pride leader."

He stretched his wings, a common occurrence after a day of hunting with his other children. "But if there's one thing you can be sure of, it's that the easy times don't stick around for long. If you can only catch eel when they're plentiful, you'll starve when they're not."

He looked his daughter in the eye. Even from across the room, he commanded attention. "If you can survive in the aneda forests on our border with the taiga, you can survive anywhere, Satra. That's why I put you there, so you could learn to survive. Because that's what it means to be kjarr."

"To be kjarr is to survive," she echoed. She'd heard those words often but never from her father before now.

"Yes, to be kjarr is to survive," he said, "but if this is too difficult for you, I can reassign you to help your brother or Vitra in the bog. I didn't intend for this to be punishment. I didn't intend to cause you shame."

Satra thought of Mignet's big blue eyes when they touched beaks and her nares blushed red. Across from Satra was her father, a gryphon she didn't think had ever groomed her, even when she was a gryphlet. "No, pride leader, I'll learn to hunt in the aneda forests. I'll learn to fly in the cold air. I won't quit."

Jun softened. He lowered his head slightly for her. "If you need anything, I'm always available to you. If you have any questions, you can ask me anytime."

Satra didn't correct his lie. She'd swung by his nest every day for a month and not run into him once. She never knew where he was. "Father, why didn't Vitra have to hunt in the aneda forests?"

"You're not your sister, Satra," Jun said. "You shouldn't

compare yourself to her. She's had a hard life. But to answer your question, her mother's a bog gryphon, and she wanted to explore the deep bog. I thought that was what she needed most at the time. Some gryphons are born with grit and some need to learn it. Your sister could survive the Connixation. You had yet to learn to survive on your own."

"Yes, Father." It would be easier for Satra not to compare herself to her sister if everyone else would stop, her father included.

Jun looked to the back of the den, where Thenca and her twin brother stood guard. "Thenca, are you still hunting north of the river?"

"Yes, Kjarr," Thenca said.

Jun stood. "Excellent. Take Satra with you for the next few days. Teach her how to hunt. While I'm happy she hasn't starved, I'd like to see her start bringing back food for the rest of the pride. Make it happen."

Jun exited the den, leaving Satra alone with Thenca and Urious. Even having been around them for her entire life, she still had to look for Urious's tail scars to tell them apart as they came over to comfort her.

"Are you sure you want to stay in the cold and aneda?" Urious asked. "There's no shame in hunting in the kjarr. Only you and your brother have ever been assigned to the aneda forests right after fledging."

"How did my brother do?" Satra asked.

"Terrible." Thenca said. "He was the worst. I don't know that he caught anything while there was still snow on the ground except for a cold."

"But... why does my father love him best, then?" Satra asked.

"The same way you needed grit, your brother needed love," Urious said. When Satra looked like she needed love,

Urious used his mockingbird voice to mimic Jun. "Satra, you are the best. Vitra is a conceited eel who can't fly half as well as you can. And your brother is clingy. You are my favorite child."

Satra laughed in spite of herself.

"Come along, it's time to get some sleep," Thenca said. "I've picked up a lot of tricks hunting in the northern forest. I'll show you how to catch prey there. I'm somewhat of an expert."

You picked up a lot of tricks from your owl gryphon lover, Satra thought, but she didn't say it out loud. If Thenca didn't want the pride to know about her and Deracho, Satra wouldn't say anything. But that did give Satra an idea. If Thenca could learn to hunt in the aneda forests from Deracho, maybe Satra could learn from Mignet.

Assuming Mignet doesn't abandon me while I'm stuck up north with Thenca.

BY THE TIME Satra got back to her own hunting grounds, Mignet was nowhere to be found. Thenca had given her a few pointers, so Satra got to work trying to track frost chickens in the snow. At least, Thenca called them frost chickens. Satra thought they looked like swamp grouse.

She'd just managed to locate, chase, and lose her first frost chicken when she saw a shape landing on the icy lake. Mignet looked around, but didn't see Satra on the shoreline.

Mignet was about to leave when Satra shouted, "Hey, over here!"

The taiga gryphon started, then turned and followed the voice. "I thought you'd abandoned me. I was just about to siege the kjarr nesting grounds and beat up all two thousand kjarr gryphons until I found you."

Mignet looked Satra in the eyes, though this time she didn't touch her beak to Satra's. There was something off about Mignet, and it took Satra a few minutes before she realized it.

"Your eyes," Satra said. "They're not the same shade of blue."

"Oh?" Mignet asked. "I can't see my own eyes, but I noticed there's some green in Younce's. I guess the blue-eyed winter has finally come to an end."

"Your eyes are only blue for winter?" Satra's voice was skeptical. She'd never heard of such a thing.

"It's true." Mignet put her eyes up to Satra's, touching her beak this time. "By the time spring is done, my eyes will be back to their normal color."

"What's their real color?" Satra asked.

"How should I know?" Mignet said. "You're the one always looking into them."

Satra put a wing around her taiga crush. "But why do they change? What's the point? Is it to help you attract a mate?"

"Is it working?" Mignet batted her eyelashes. "It helps me see at night. When the days are short and my eyes are blue, I can still see after the sun goes down. By the time summer comes and my eyes are their normal color, the night is just as dark for me as it is for you."

Satra shook her head. "I don't have any magical powers like that."

"That's not true," Mignet chided. "You can slide across the ice on your paws. That's pretty fantastic. Want to go ice sliding?"

Satra did, but she had a more important use for the last

of the daylight. "We can later, but first, can you teach me how to hunt up here?"

HUNTING LESSONS TOOK SEVERAL DAYS. Most of what Mignet told Satra were the same things Thenca had said. Presumably, both had been taught by Deracho. What surprised Satra, however, was just how bad at hunting Mignet was.

Her technique was good right up until the moment she had to pounce. Then, her poor aim cost her the kill. Watching her grow frustrated and even angry, Satra realized she'd never actually seen Mignet catch anything except the first frog Satra had driven onto the ice.

When Mignet became despondent, Satra would sit next to her in the snow and wrap her wing around her friend. Sometimes, they'd go ice sliding first, Mignet pushing Satra around. Then they'd crash into the snow and dry off on their favorite boulder. Other times, Mignet helped Satra practice her flying. She was starting to get pretty good at it.

"I'm terrible at hunting," Mignet said one afternoon when not even ice sliding had improved her mood. "I'm just useless as a gryphon."

"Well, it's a good thing you're so pretty and smart," Satra said.

Mignet sighed. "What use is a smart taiga gryphon? What am I going to do, invent a new type of snow?"

"With just fifty gryphons, you could be the den mother," Satra said. "Do taiga gryphons have a den mother? How are you at laying eggs? I'll bet your father wants you to hatch a whole pride's worth of plague-resistant gryphlets."

Mignet swatted her beak. "I don't want to lay eggs. Or have to deal with gryphlets. Or the weirdness that comes with meeting someone, mating, and never seeing them again unless the egg hatches and the hatchling is like a parrotface or fantail and you have to find a new home for it."

"Hmm," Satra said, but Mignet had turned serious.

The taiga gryphon pushed her face up against Satra's again. "Are you trying to get rid of me? We could run away together and become fisherfolk. We already shared a nest together!"

"Whoa, what?" Satra asked. "We built a nest together. That's not the same thing!"

"Yes, run away and build a nest with me!" Mignet said with a laugh. "Catching fish can't be harder than catching chickens. Don't you want to be a fisherfolk?"

"There's no such thing as fisherfolk," Satra protested.

Mignet stopped and blinked. "Of course there are."

"I went to the shore south of the kjarr," Satra said. "There weren't any fisherfolk there."

"They're on the other side, the weald side," Mignet said.

"Have you ever *seen* a fisherfolk?" Satra stood defiant.

"Well, sort of?" Mignet's ears turned sideways while she thought. "I flew down past the abandoned nesting grounds with my father last autumn. Down at the southern edge of the taiga, we saw some gryphons and opinici flying around above the dunes. I guess they were fisherfolk."

"Pshaw," Satra protested. "Until you prove to me that fisherfolk exist, I'm not running away with you. Not to the shore, not to anywhere."

"What about to the hot springs?" Mignet said. Her eyes sparkled with a hint of purple.

"I thought you said your pride leader father wouldn't want a kjarr gryphon up there?" Satra's anxiety rose.

Mignet's tailfeathers twitched back and forth. "They

don't have to know. We can sneak in at night and use the ones near my cave."

"I'm not sure." Satra pawed at the snow. "I don't think I can fly through the mountains at night. It's too dark."

Mignet pointed to her eyes. "They're still mostly blue, right? I can guide you. Once they lose their color, we lose our chance."

Satra hesitated.

"Come on!" Mignet said. "What's the worst that happens? We get scolded and you're sent home? I'll bet Thenca sneaks into Deracho's cave every night."

Thenca had been working on her late night hunting skills a lot lately. Even Urious was getting suspicious.

"Okay, fine," Mignet sighed. "I will abandon our dream of becoming fisherfolk. We will forever just be hunting friends, not secret opinicus life mates."

"I'll go." Satra surprised herself and Mignet with the words. "They all think Thenca hunts better in the aneda forest at night, so I'll tell them I'm going to try night hunting with her. Then tomorrow night, I'll meet you here."

"Promise?" Mignet asked.

"I promise," Satra said. She pounced Mignet off the boulder and back into the snow.

THE NIGHT of her Snowfall infiltration, Satra's plan ran into one small problem. For the first time in a month, Thenca didn't slip away to see Deracho. Instead, she stayed in her own nest. While Satra worried someone might notice and call her bluff, in the end, no one really cared how she spent her time. She slipped out of the nesting grounds and made her way through the dark to the frozen lake where Mignet was waiting.

"This is going to be tricky. The air currents can get pretty bad near the mountains," Mignet said. "I'm going to take the safest route, not the fastest route, and we'll stop a couple of times to relax. We'll take it nice and easy, okay?"

Satra nodded. Her adrenaline was already pumping, though some of that was the thought of spending the evening with Mignet.

Mignet cuddled up against Satra. "Our first stop is that mountain in the distance. Can you see it?"

Satra shook her head. "I can't see anything except you, 'cause you're all white."

"Okay, well, you just keep your eyes on me, and I'll chirp when it's time to take a break," Mignet said. "Sound good?"

"Sounds good," Satra confirmed. She flew after Mignet. Satra's wings ached in the cold, but she kept her eyes on the rosettes on Mignet's flank, and over time, her wings began to warm up. She was starting to feel pretty good when Mignet called for their first break.

The tops of the mountains were free of aneda trees, so they flew down and found a small grove to rest in. The trees kept the winds away, but without the exertion of flying, Satra cooled off quickly.

Mignet took some dried, salted meat out of her pouch and handed it to Satra. "Here, you should eat something. It's salty, but our next stop has water."

When Satra shivered, Mignet wrapped herself around her kjarr friend.

"Is it much farther?" Satra's beak chattered in the cold.

"Nope, just one more stop between us and Snowfall." Mignet's ears perked up. Down the hill, not far from where they were resting, came the *mronks* of several large, predatory birds. "We should get going. We don't want to get caught off guard by a goliath. They're a lot more likely to attack a gryphon this time of year."

Goliath birds were huge, larger than the tallest gryphon. There were several types, all flightless, but the feral breed that stalked the taiga was the most vicious. Satra still dreamed of killing one with Mignet's help and bringing it home to feed her pride, but she wasn't sure how a small gryphon took down something that big.

They spent a little longer cuddling at the final stop before Snowfall. This time, they had fresh water and a cave to rest in.

With the snow barrier up, Satra couldn't see anything. "How do you know where the water is?"

"I left the entrance open a crack," Mignet said. "My eyes are losing a little of their night vision, and the daytime is a little clearer now, but I can still make out the interior here."

Something that had been sticking in the back of Satra's mind finally found its place with the words *and the daytime is a little clearer now*. Was the reason Mignet was such a bad hunter because she couldn't see during the day?

While she couldn't bring herself to come out and ask Mignet about it, Satra was certain she'd struck on the truth. Mignet was coming out during the day to hunt so she could be closer to Satra just like Thenca was going out at night to spend time with Deracho. All of the other taiga pride probably hunted after dark except for Mignet. It also explained why she had no sense of personal space. She couldn't see Satra's facial expressions unless they were touching.

Satra felt flush. "I think I'm warm enough. Let's head to Snowfall, shall we?"

THE TAIGA NESTING grounds were a glacier-formed amphitheater atop Snowfall Mountain. At least, that's what Satra had been told. In the dark, she couldn't make out much of anything. Several times, Mignet hid Satra away while she spoke with patrols or groups of taiga gryphons heading out to hunt. Even Deracho made an appearance. He gathered several others to help him fly a dead goliath bird up the mountain.

Then there came a moment where the common area cleared, and Mignet pulled Satra out of her hiding spot and into a cavern. While the moonlight had given her the general outline of the amphitheater, she couldn't see anything in the dark and stumbled a few times.

"Shh, keep it down," Mignet whispered. "My dad's quarters are at the end of the passageway, just past mine. I don't want him hearing us."

Satra wanted to protest that she was being as silent as she could be under the circumstances, but she decided part of being quiet was keeping her beak shut. The passage became humid and warm before splitting in two directions.

Mignet pulled Satra into a side room. Satra could feel her dry fur soaking up the moisture. There was a thin layer of cool water on the floor.

"Careful now," Mignet said. "We're just about there. It's probably a little easier for you to back into the water so you can feel the bottom."

Satra allowed herself to be positioned backwards. She took a step down. Her tail touched the top of the water, and she jumped straight up.

"It's hot," she whispered. "Hotter than a lake in summer."

Mignet laughed, stuffing one paw into her mouth to

keep from waking up anyone in the side caves. "Of course it's hot. It's a hot spring!"

Satra knew it was a hot spring, but she hadn't realized just how hot it would be. She heard Mignet slide into the water.

Mignet grabbed Satra's back half and helped lower her down. "See, here's the edge. It's only a few gryphon lengths across in each direction. You can hang onto it if you want. Or me, if that's easier. Do you know how to swim?"

"A little," Satra said. There were some springs that fed into the Kjarr River she sometimes practiced in. The water there was icy. She stretched down until her paws touched the bottom. She could hear the sound of water flowing from somewhere higher down into the pool.

"Not so bad, is it?" Mignet put her paws over Satra's and guided her along the edge.

Satra was starting to relax. All of her anxiety over hunting slipped away, followed by her worries over how she'd get back home later. She put her paws on Mignet's shoulder, then traced them up to her face. She pushed her beak against Mignet's and still couldn't see her.

"Hey," Mignet said.

"Hey yourself," Satra replied.

Satra was so caught up in Mignet that she didn't realize the scratching sounds she was hearing from the passageway were other gryphons until it was too late.

Two strangers stumbled into the hot springs with a splash.

"We found it!" one said.

"Shh, keep it down or you might wake Mignet or her father!" the other scolded.

Mignet and Satra both froze. When one of the strangers bumped into Satra, however, she let out a squeak of fright.

The two intruding gryphons let out their own squeaks, much louder than Satra's.

"Mignet?!" one voice exclaimed. "Who's there with you? Why're her feathers so dark?"

"Younce and Zeph, you two ruin everything!" Mignet shouted back.

From farther down the cavern came a deeper voice. "What's going on down there? You fledglings aren't sneaking into the hot springs at night again, are you? I'll have the den mother shave you bare if I catch you in there again!"

Mignet pulled Satra out of the water and pushed her up the cavern. "Go hide!"

Mignet turned back in time to block the two intruders from getting out. "Dad! I caught Zeph and Younce in the springs again!"

By their groans, they weren't happy to have been thrown under the pride leader's paws by Mignet, but it kept her dad from going all the way up the passage. Satra tried to sneak out, but she was soaked through to her undercoat. She reached the top of the cave but couldn't see anything. She flapped her wings a few times but didn't get any lift. She was starting to shiver when a white blur appeared in front of her.

"Satra?" the owl gryphon hooted. "Thenca's Satra?"

She nodded. At least, she tried to nod. It came across as more of an exaggerated shiver.

"This way, quickly. We'll get you dry enough to fly." He moved up to her side and began to guide her. "I'm Deracho. I've seen you sleeping in Thenca's nest the few times I've escorted her home. She's going to kill you when she finds out you snuck into Snowfall."

Satra wanted to ask him not to tell Thenca, but her body temperature was dropping fast. He led her into a different cave and secured the weather barrier. He pushed her against something warm. By the smell, it was another dead goliath bird, though newly so. He groomed the water out of her feathers and let her eat.

It took a few hours until she was dry, then another hour before a break in the patrols came. Unlike Mignet, Deracho didn't let her stop to take a break. Her wings hurt terribly by the time she got back to her own nesting grounds.

SATRA'S BLACK-BACKED ears burned from the scolding Thenca gave her. The angry bog gryphon had threatened every kind of punishment imaginable if Satra ever snuck into Snowfall again, but she promised not to tell Satra's father.

That didn't stop Thenca from hissing her disapproval at Satra all day while Satra tried to catch naps. Despite her long flight and sleepless night, Thenca wasn't about to let Satra get any rest.

In the end, Satra finally gave up and went out to pretend to hunt in the aneda forests. Mignet was nowhere in sight, and Satra was too embarrassed to know what she'd say to the taiga gryphon. She ended up finding a thicket of trees where no one would see her taking a nap, dragged her first, sticky attempt at making a nest inside the thicket, and settled atop it.

She chose this location because several aneda trees had grown into each other. Some frost chickens or perhaps a young goliath bird had burrowed through the underbrush and cleared out a spot at the center of the grove. There was only one way in or out—and not much room to maneuver once you were inside—but it would keep her away from prying eyes for a while.

She felt like she'd slept for hours when the sound of a twig snapping woke her. She opened her eyes and looked around. Mignet was coming through the branches, following Satra's trail by scent in the bright daylight.

"I'm over here," Satra began, but Mignet hissed at her to be quiet.

The taiga gryphon's fur was standing on edge. Satra sniffed, but she could only smell the bitter aneda resin. Her ears perked up, but she heard only the wind.

Mignet took a few steps closer. Behind her, the chicken burrow that led into the branches turned dark.

"It smells like goliath birds outside," the taiga gryphon whispered. "We should get out of here. The branches are too close together to climb up and fly."

Satra kept looking past Mignet, where the light wasn't coming through the pathway anymore. "Did you bring Deracho with you?"

"Deracho? No, why?" Mignet turned and saw the tunnel was blocked by a massive beak. When it breathed out, they could smell carrion on its breath.

"It's too big to get in here, right?" Satra asked. By the size of its beak, it wasn't an adolescent. It was probably a good ten feet tall.

"I don't know. It could chew its way in here." Mignet's breathing picked up. With the light blocked, her eyes found their focus again.

"How do you hunt goliath birds?" Satra asked. "I saw a few dead ones at Snowfall. You have to know how to kill one, right?"

The beak began chewing at the edges of the path through the thicket, making it bigger.

Mignet interposed herself between Satra and the giant bird. "The only plan from the ground is to get in the air. Quick movements cause them to attack, so you can use your tail to distract them. That's all I've got."

Satra began to push the sticky aneda nest into a ball. "Maybe we can shove this in its mouth and run past it?"

Mignet didn't answer. She was sniffing the air again. "This isn't the same one I smelled outside."

Satra was going to ask if it mattered, but suddenly the thick underbrush began to shake and angry *mronks* came from all directions. Above them, a beak pushed through the branches and screeched.

Mignet and Satra got behind the nest and pushed it as hard as they could. They were lucky, and the bird chewing its way through their passageway had its mouth open when the tangle of aneda branches hit. It reared back coughing, and the two gryphons escaped into the sunlight.

The weather had started to warm. While Mignet was able to get into the air, Satra's feet couldn't find purchase in the slush. She started to run away, but the goliath bird caught her with a kick and sent her flying into the nearest aneda tree.

Sharp, sticky branches tore through her flight feathers on both wings. Satra didn't bother trying to get airborne. There was no point. Instead, she ran towards the frozen lake.

The main goliath bird finished coughing up the nest, and the others, probably its offspring, pulled their heads out of the tangle and chased after her.

Where gryphons on the ground were built for skulking and pouncing, goliath birds were made for speed. Satra barely reached the edge of the lake ahead of them. She could hear her taiga beloved shouting down at her, trying to figure out what Satra's plan was.

Satra didn't have a plan, exactly. It was more of a hunch. She dove onto the lake, letting its slick surface carry her across. The four goliath birds chasing after her hit the ice and didn't have traction. They fell down and slid after her, their momentum causing them to gain on her.

Just when she thought they'd catch up to her, a flash of white and black dove down behind her and began to push.

"Hold on tight," Mignet said. Satra gained speed, but despite Mignet's best efforts, the goliath birds were still gaining on them.

"Use your tailfeathers," Satra shouted.

Mignet laughed, then managed to turn Satra right as the first goliath bird slipped past them, lashing out with its beak and talons and leaving long cracks in the ice where the gryphon couple had just been.

Once they were on their own trajectory, Mignet got them safely to the shore.

"Thanks for the rescue." Satra nuzzled Mignet.

The taiga gryphon looked over Satra's shredded wings. "Are they broken? Do you think you can fly? We don't want to be here when the birds get back to solid ground."

Satra preened a few twigs out of her feathers. They were sticky enough that she decided it was better to let a medicine gryphon deal with them later. She was too likely to pull out her feathers by accident.

Several angry *mronks* cried out from the middle of the lake.

"Never mind, I don't think they're going to reach the shore." Mignet giggled. "They look pretty stuck from here."

Satra wanted nothing more than to rest here with Mignet,

but something occurred to her. "You said you didn't know how to hunt a goliath bird from the ground. Now that you can fly, how would you do it? Four goliath birds is a lot of meat."

"Hmmm." Mignet's tailfeathers twitched back and forth while she thought. "I have a few ideas, but hunting goliaths is usually something you do in groups of three or four."

"Thenca was still awake when I came out here," Satra said. "Do you know where Deracho hunts? They're probably out there now talking about us."

One of the goliath birds tried to stand up but fell onto its stomach. Satra was sympathetic, having been in that position before herself. The ice was much slicker than it had been even a few days past.

"Okay, I'll go fetch them," Mignet said at last. "You find a tree to climb in case they squirm their way to the shore."

IT TOOK Mignet an hour to locate Thenca and Deracho, during which time Satra climbed the tallest tree she could find and kept watch on the birds. One had nearly reached the shore by the time Deracho and Thenca arrived.

While Mignet and Thenca used branches or rocks to distract the sharp goliath beaks, Deracho landed on the ice behind them and latched onto the back of their necks, killing them with a single bite. Once all four were dispatched, the gryphons pulled them onto the shore.

"We should get help from Snowfall to carry these," Mignet said, but the two mature gryphons shared a look.

"Zeph and Younce told your father you'd been sneaking kjarr gryphons into the springs," Deracho said. "You'll probably be punished tonight, especially if he finds out you've been out here hunting with the same kjarr gryphon you smuggled into the pride leader's private hot springs."

Thenca cleaned some of the blood from Deracho's face before turning to Mignet. "But if you bring back two goliath birds on your own and don't mention Satra's part in it, he'll probably forgive last night's trespasses. Though if you don't mind helping us take our two down the mountain, that'd be much appreciated."

Satra wanted to celebrate their shared kill together, but she didn't want Mignet to get into trouble on her behalf. The taiga gryphon's eyes had a hint of purple in them as their natural color began to show through the blue. They worked together to carry one of the smaller goliath birds down the mountain while Deracho and Thenca dragged the larger one. Only once they were near the river did Deracho fly back to Snowfall to fetch help for the other two kills.

Thenca flew off to find a kjarr patrol to help carry their two kills to the nesting grounds leaving Satra to sit and daydream about Mignet. They made a good team, but there was something more to it. Maybe it was that Mignet was half-opinicus and they mated for life, but Satra could see herself spending the rest of her adulthood with Mignet by her side. And, unless she was reading the signs wrong, she thought Mignet felt the same.

By the time Thenca and a patrol returned for the goliath birds, Satra had made up her mind. She'd tell Mignet how she felt tomorrow, and they'd figure out what to do about it from there. Maybe Mignet was right and fisherfolk were real. If so, they could run off and be fisherfolk together. Satra had several siblings who could take over as pride leader if something happened to her father. And Mignet...

Here Satra realized she might have a problem. Mignet hadn't mentioned any siblings. She was one of the only gryphons born of a plague survivor. The plague was a big deal east of the kjarr, and she was one of four gryphons who might have inherited a resistance to it. It wasn't just her pride leader father; *everyone* would expect her to have gryphlets.

Satra shook her head. It didn't matter. She'd tell Mignet tomorrow and let her make the choice.

AFTER A NIGHT of celebration and goliath bird meat, Satra was feeling sluggish the next morning. The medicine gryphons had managed to get the twigs and branches out of her wings. A few feathers had been lost or broken, but the medicine gryphons imped new ones in. Despite unfounded fears that she'd never fly again, they'd called her overly dramatic and just asked her to wait a few days before going airborne. Thus Satra, Daughter of the Kjarr, walked through the melting slush to her hunting grounds.

Mignet was waiting for her along the shore of the frozen lake. The sun was already shining, a sign that spring now held sway over winter, and Satra could see where the goliath birds had nearly broken through the ice.

Mignet bounded over and ruffled Satra's crest of golden feathers. Her violet eyes were striking. Another few days and Satra might find out what Mignet's real eye color was. She returned the taiga gryphon's affection, preening her feathers and taking in her dry mountain scent.

Satra wanted to speak, but the words didn't come. More than her family—both biological and her actual caretakers, Thenca and Urious—Mignet had become someone Satra couldn't imagine being without. The thought of not seeing Mignet each day was like the thought of her wings never healing; it was unthinkable. With stakes so high, she couldn't make her beak work to tell Mignet of her plans.

Finally, Mignet grew agitated at having Satra staring at her looking like she was going to speak. "What is it? Did you get into trouble? Did Thenca tell your dad?"

Satra's beak shut with a click. She caught her breath, then tried again. "Do you want to be a fisherfolk? With me?"

Mignet's posture stiffened. "What're you asking?"

"We wouldn't have to live there," Satra backtracked, "but they probably have some sort of life mate ceremony, right? If we did that, our prides couldn't split us apart."

Mignet's ears were back, a bad sign. "Where would we live? I'd melt in the kjarr summer, and you'd freeze during the taiga winter."

"We could live right here on the border in the aneda forest." Satra's heart sank. She'd expected jubilation or rejection, not nitpicking. "Or we could stay in the kjarr during the winter and the taiga in the summer."

"Hmmm." Mignet's left ear twitched. She kneaded the snow while Satra waited for a response.

Satra was starting to think this was a mistake. The more time she had to live in her own mind, however, the less she thought that. She couldn't keep going out hunting with Mignet as a friend. It would drive her mad. However things turned out, it was better to know.

"Okay," Mignet said at last.

Satra wasn't sure what she meant.

Mignet stood. "Let's do it. I've never heard of two gryphons joining the fisherfolk just to be life mated or whatever and then returning home, but what's the worst our fathers can do, tell us no? If my dad thinks there's a real possibility I might leave to join the fisherfolk forever, he's going to cave."

Satra thought her father was just as likely to give in, but only because he had other children he loved best. She didn't know what to say to Mignet, so she squealed and pounced her instead.

Mignet laughed. "Just give me a few days for my eyes to change to their summer color, then we'll meet here and head south. I'll leave a message with Younce and Zeph and make them promise not to tell anyone until a day has passed. They may worry, but they won't catch us in time!"

With their future ahead of them, there was no chance either of them would get any hunting done this afternoon. They laughed and played in the melting aneda forest, splashing through slush and startling defrosting frogs and molting frost chickens.

Satra chased Mignet, who stayed just out of reach with her beautiful white wings spread. The black bars of adolescence were finally fading from her plumage. The light caught on the silver bracelet her opinicus mother had given her. The world felt brighter and warmer than it ever had before.

Their play led them to the edge of the frozen lake where they'd first met. Mignet landed on its slick surface, daring Satra to come out to catch her. Satra tried to warn her that the ice was thin, but the moment her paws hit the lake, she began to slide.

Mignet backed up, but the blue in her eyes didn't let her see where the goliath birds had cracked the ice. Just as the weight of Satra and Mignet hit the same spot, it all gave way.

On the first day of a warm spring in the aneda forests of the taiga, a small silver bracelet with a blue heron engraved upon it settled upon the bottom of the frigid lake.

CONNIXATION

"Tell me the story of the Connixation again, Ti." Cici, still downy despite the late spring, chirped up at his sister.

The sun was bright and the day was warm. Tielle looked out from the top of Williwaw Mountain at her friends playing in the skies above. Then she looked back at the pride's nesting grounds, empty except for herself and her younger, late-blooming brother.

"Are you sure?" she asked. "It's a scary story."

He nodded enthusiastically, looking like a snowball with a beak wobbling up and down.

She sighed and settled down in the warm nest next to him. He'd be able to fly soon, then she wouldn't get stuck playing makeshift den mother. "Okay, Ci, have it your way. This is the story of how the world ends..."

BLACK ASH COATED WILLIWAW MOUNTAIN. The southernmost taiga pride, once bright and white, were all stained a volcanic grey. Soon after the ash fell, the coughing began.

Tielle shivered. It was two years since she'd last felt

warm. She shoveled another foot of dark snow out of the cave entrance. Her paws were stained black. Shadowy footprints led in and out of the single cavern nesting grounds.

They were the smallest of the taiga prides and had only the single medicine gryphon. She'd warned that grooming the ash out of their fur would lead to the cough, but no one had found a way to get clean without preening. Gryphon feathers and fur just weren't built to function any other way. Early into the volcanic winter, the Williwaw Pride had gone north to Hoarfrost to borrow their hot springs. Now, the springs were stained as black as those who used them.

A few gryphons had snuck down to the ocean. There was a small fishing outpost set up along the dunes. As the temperatures continued dropping, even the coastal waters had frozen all the way out to the closest islands.

More coughing drew Tielle out of her mental snow-gathering. All of their food was covered in ash, so even the gryphons with enough willpower to stop grooming were starting to fall sick. One way or another, everyone was ingesting it.

In the east, in the weald, a thick canopy of redwood forest kept the tainted snow off the ground. From the southern edge where the fantails and feathermanes lived up to the northern tip where a group of opinici had set up a city, massive trees blanketed the valley.

The mountain prides didn't have it so easy. Despite the lowest temperatures in memory, patrols and messengers flowed up and down the mountain range, bringing news from the Snowfeather Highlands, Snowfall, Hoarfrost, and the other taiga prides. There was a slow-moving snow-storm due to reach the highlands any day now. While fast moving blizzards offered their own dangers, the worst storms were the ones that stalled over the mountains.

Those were the ones that didn't just kill gryphons, they ended prides.

More coughing. Tielle shook out her fur and feathers as best she could manage. This was her last chance to go down into the weald to trade for medicine. Once the blizzard was overhead, they could be stuck inside a single cavern for weeks.

The Williwaw pride leader had told her she had to stop running from her problems and face them head on. Not that there was anywhere to run to now—all that existed south of them was water. She looked down the cliffs to the shelf of ice below. Cici had loved the ocean.

She steeled herself before leaping into the sky and gliding to the feathermane nesting grounds.

THE SUN SHONE over the taiga. Tielle chased her now-fledged brother through the warm air currents along the cliffs. Their feathers were a bright white against the blue of the ocean.

Cici ducked under a branch, pushed off of an outcropping, and charged back at her. She let out a playful roar, startling a nest of gyrfalcons who chirped for their mother.

With a laugh, they let the small bird chase them away from the cliffs below Williwaw and north towards Hoarfrost for their next adventure. The world was so warm, so bright, so clean.

BELOW THE FROZEN CANOPY, the temperatures were comfortable for Tielle with her thick feathers and fur. Unfortunately, what was comfortable for a Williwaw gryphon was dangerously cold for any weald inhabitant.

The feathermane nesting grounds were full of other prides seeking to trade for goldmint, the only herb that helped against the black cough. Copper hawks, magpies, saberbeaks, and parrotfaces filled the forest with their chirps. They all had food to trade, but Tielle only had aneda resin. It was useful for bites and scratches but useless against what afflicted her pride now.

She pushed her way through the crowd. Several gryphons balked at the grey smudges she left on their fur as she slid past them. The Feathermane Pride's leader, Blue-mane, was talking to several parrotfaces, so she waited her turn. By the time she was able to speak, he was already frowning at her.

"I've never seen a dark-coated taiga gryphon before." His words came at a rumble. His azure mane looked pristine next to hers. "Snowfeather?"

She shook her head. "Williwaw. I've come to trade for medicine. The black cough has hit most of my pridemates. I have aneda resin. Come spring, there are always hunting injuries."

"I'm sorry, but we're already stocked." He looked at her with pity. "The Hoarfrost Pride came before you. We have enough to last us for years. You don't have any sugar frogs with you, do you?"

"No, they're all buried under a goliath bird's height of snow until spring." She drooped down. In the current weather conditions, it was a long flight to come back empty-pawed. Most of her pride wouldn't survive the blizzard without medicine.

"You might have better luck with the fantails," Bluemane continued. "They left a few moments ago, dragging their goods behind them. One of their traders, Golrin Goldpaw, found a patch of goldmint and came here looking to make a deal. He came away with a lot of monitor meat from the saberbeaks and a couple of parrots from the copper hawks, but there weren't any taiga gryphons here at the time. He probably doesn't have any aneda."

Tielle thanked the pride leader for his time. While he moved on to the next set of concerns, she made the calculations in her head.

You can't run from your problems this time, Tielle. The pride needs you. Their lives are in your paws.

If she caught the fantail traders before they reached their home, she might still get back to Williwaw before it became too cold to fly. Bluemane said they'd been dragging goods behind them, so they weren't flying.

She exited the nesting grounds and shook as much ash off as she could. Behind her, she could hear a magpie commenting on the coal-colored footprints she'd left behind with her big paws.

THE WARM SKIES above Hoarfrost were too crowded for Cici. A hundred white, rosetted gryphons filled the skies. He'd fledged late and loved to fly like he was making up for lost time.

Tielle chirped a greeting to one of her friends, Matri, as she and her brother flew overhead, promising to swing by on their way home. Cici was looking for something specific that day, a stretch of hot springs along the kjarr border.

"Slow down, wait for me!" she shouted at him, but he just kept flying.

She frowned. If they didn't locate the springs soon, there wouldn't be time to fly all the way home. They could stay with the Snowfall or Hoarfrost prides, but their den mother would worry.

"I think I see it, Ti!" Below Cici, on the kjarr side of the aneda forest, there was a small break in the trees with a river running out of it.

TIELLE FOLLOWED the signs of gryphons dragging large prey through the snow and underbrush. With their head start, it still took her an hour to catch up. She found the fantail traders but not in the state she was expecting. The snow was stained with blood.

Six fantails were bleeding out. Their goods had all been stolen. There was no chance the thieves had taken the food and not also checked for goldmint.

Even though aneda was the only valuable thing she had to trade, she didn't hesitate. She pulled out the poultices, prepared by the Williwaw medicine gryphon, and started to patch up the wounded.

Fantails could resemble most of the other gryphon prides, with one crucial difference: they always had long, feathered tails. It was extremely rare to find a gryphon with a feathered tail outside of the fantails. Only the fisherfolk and opinici shared that trait.

The first gryphon she tried to patch up had only superficial wounds, and when she saw Tielle's dark fur and plumage, she cried out, "Padfeet! They're back!"

"I'm not a padfoot," Tielle explained. "I'm just covered in ash. Stay still while I fix you up."

It took more of her precious time, but she stopped the bleeding on the worst of the wounded. "What happened here? You said you were attacked by padfeet? Who's in charge here?"

A padfoot was a gryphon who turned their back on their pride to become a thief. Occasionally, a group of padfeet would become large enough to form their own pride. They rarely had nesting grounds, instead moving from location to location to keep from being attacked when they caused too much trouble.

Before the ash, there were no padfeet in the weald or taiga. Before the ash, there'd been enough food and medicine to go around.

"Golrin," one of the wounded said. She was the first one Tielle had patched up, and she was already back on her feet. "They took him with the supplies. They want him to take them to where he found the goldmint."

"There's no hidden patch of goldmint," another explained. "He was clearing out the winter nests and came across a stash of dried herbs in the back of a cave. We figured now was the time to trade it."

"They're going to kill him when they find out," the first fantail said. "You have to save him. If you can locate them and fly to the nearest nests, the fantails will come help you. Please, you have to help!"

You can't run forever.

Tielle looked over the traders. While she'd stopped the bleeding and gotten them back on their feet, none of them would be much good in a fight. Because the padfeet had taken the heavy monitor meat, she could see drag marks headed north towards Glacial Run.

"Okay, I'll do it," she said. "You head east and get backup for me. I'll do what I can to find them before they kill your friend."

She beaked through her harness and emptied out the last of the aneda medicines. This bunch would need it if their wounds reopened on the way. She kept one set for

Golrin. Depending on how good of a liar he was, he could already be wounded and dying.

CICI PULLED *his tail out of the river. "It's definitely warmer here than it was downstream."*

Tielle was skeptical. Her brother had a way of seeing what he wanted to see.

She dipped a paw into the water. "It does seem warmer than it should be."

There was a hesitation in her voice. Cici had a way of convincing other gryphons he was right. Was the water really warmer?

"It must be the secret kjarr hot springs," he said. "What else could it be?"

She shrugged. "Maybe a monitor peed in the river upstream."

She hadn't meant it as a joke, but he laughed and laughed.

"Keep it down!" she scolded. "The kjarr gryphons won't appreciate finding us here."

"You should be less funny if you don't want me to laugh." His voice had a hint of songbird so both his kind words and laughter sounded the same.

She looked upstream. The cave disappeared into the mountain face. "It's too dark. I've lost the blue in my eyes."

He nuzzled her. "I'll be your eyes."

Late to fledge, late to get his winter vision, late to lose the blue. Her brother was late for everything. There was just the barest hint of purple in the eyes that begged her to explore a little further with him.

"Okay," she said. "We'll go inside. Let's find this spring and head home."

Brother and sister followed the water as it disappeared into the mountain's dark maw.

TIELLE HAD one advantage over the pack of padfeet she was pursuing: they were upwind from her. Even in winter, she was used to tracking things by smell.

Three times now, she'd reached a clearing and had to trust her nares to find the scent. Only once had she been forced to backtrack and try again. She needed to locate them soon, as the cliffs overlooking Glacial Run were coming up. If they took to flying, she wouldn't be able to track them.

Luck didn't appear to be on her side. The scent led to the ledge. Down below, the river was frozen solid. She walked to the edge and sniffed around. The scent, mostly dead monitor but also a hint of harpy eagle and fresh mint, didn't appear any stronger in a particular direction.

She looked west, to the taiga.

You have to stop running from your problems. You have to stand and fight. You need to be an adult. Have you learned nothing from your brother?

There was nowhere to go. She slumped down, and the scent picked up the tiniest bit. She sniffed and stuck her head over the side. The scent trail went down the cliff towards a cave. During the summer, when the river was at its height, the entrance would have been underwater.

Her pulse quickened. Even the enclosed space of the Williwaw nesting grounds caused her anxiety now. The pride leader's words of wisdom—also a threat—stuck with her. If she came back without any medicine, would they disown her? Would the fisherfolk take her in, or would she find herself a padfoot? She pushed aside her feelings and flew down to the ice.

The frozen river around the cave entrance had been cleared, but a layer of black snow coated the rest. She started to take a step towards the opening when a cry for help came from overhead.

She slunk down into the snow, letting her stained feathers camouflage her.

In the skies, several opinici fled south. Blue, green, and white, they resembled peacocks. Their cries for help echoed against the rocky sides and frozen surface of the waterway.

Farther up, diving harpy eagle gryphons forced them out of the air. The harpy gryphons had beaks that turned down at the end like icicles. They were an offshoot of the Feathermane Pride, an appearance that was only two generations old. A couple still had their feathery manes, but the rest had lost them.

One of the opinici was struck from above and crashed next to Tielle's hiding spot. While everyone's attention was on the skies, she crept over to the opinicus and crawled on top of her, spreading her wings to shield her from view.

"Keep quiet," Tielle said. "I'll keep you hidden as best I can. Are your wings broken?"

The opinicus coughed. Their body heat melted the snow, soaking her white feathers with the dark ash.

"I think my foreleg is, but my wings feel okay," the opinicus said. "Who are you? Who are they?"

"I'm Tielle of Williwaw," she responded. *At least until my pride disowns me for giving away all our aneda.* "They're padfeet, outcasts from the Feathermane Pride. They took a fantail hostage. He has medicine my pride needs. I'm going to try to free him and get it back. Who are you?"

"Li-Enn," the opinicus said. "The ash and cold has

driven the eyrie mad. We decided we were safer with the fisherfolk than waiting out the storm. The few refugees who fled south are telling stories about entire villages being found frozen solid. I'm supposed to meet a fantail trader near here."

"If it's the same trader I'm after, he's the one they caught." Tielle was about to ask what a fantail had to do with fisherfolk and opinici, but a harpy eagle cry silenced further questions. She kept the wounded opinicus hidden while the padfeet convinced the rest of the opinici to land. They were stripped of their gear and escorted into the cave.

Tielle pulled herself off of Li-Enn. "I'm going inside. I need to find Golrin. You should head south. You don't want to get caught when night falls."

The opinicus hesitated. There had been more than just a flicker of recognition at the word *Golrin*. Whatever he was to her, he was more than just a guide.

"I'll free your friends," Tielle added. When this didn't get any more of a response, she added, "If I don't come out before dark, head southeast and find a fantail. Tell them where we're at. They'll send reinforcements."

Li-Enn finally nodded and flew above the cliffs to find a safe, relatively warm place to hide. As grateful as Tielle would be for some help right now, a wounded opinicus would be more of a liability. Besides, she had an advantage over the padfeet. Unlike them, she could see in the dark.

Unlike last time.

She crawled towards the thieves' hideout, keeping close to the ground in case they had more flyers overhead.

"I*T JUST KEEPS GOING FARTHER* and farther," Cici whispered back to her.

Tielle winced as a drop of condensation fell on her head. The scrapes and bruises she'd suffered were a testament to her inability to see this deep in the cave.

"I've had enough, Ci." She was skeptical of his ability to see this deep. "Even if there is a hot spring, it's too dark down here. It'd be dangerous to use it. And we'd be cold and wet on the flight home."

"Are you sure you're a Williwaw gryphon?" he chided. "You sound more like one of the Snowfeathers right now. Where's your sense of adventure?"

Her sense of adventure was high and dry on top of a mountain somewhere, and she let him know it.

He sighed. "Okay, another fifty paces, then we'll turn back."

"Promise?" There was a touch of fear in her voice that chaffed against her pride.

"Promise. Once we know it has a hot spring, we can come back tomorrow and explore it with friends. I'm sure Matri would love to help you." He led her deeper into the cave.

The darkness had bothered her for so long that Tielle hadn't been paying attention to the warning signs her nares were sending. The cave had a strange smell to it. With all of the humidity and water-smell, it had been hard for her to notice the growing animal scent.

It wasn't bats. Hoarfrost was infested with the small, furry flyers, and she'd recognize that smell anywhere. This was a slight, sour smell.

They reached fifty paces, but before she could tell her brother it was time to turn back, he let out a squeal of excitement.

"It opens up to a huge cavern! You should see it, Ti. There's stalactites, and a bunch of pools, and..." He ran on ahead, leaving her behind.

She could just hear the sound of water falling from above into pools in the distance.

But she heard another sound. A rumbling, chuffing sound that grew in intensity and seemed to be coming from all around them.

TIELLE SLIPPED THROUGH THE CAVE, pushing thoughts of Cici from her mind lest they distract her. Her large, furry paws didn't make a sound. She passed by crates of supplies stolen from opinici. Freshwater fish, pickled salamander, and goliath jerky made her stomach rumble. Every couple of paces, there was a barrel of water treated with herbs to keep it from going sour. They smelled minty.

Too bad it isn't goldmint, she thought. But she knew that even if it were, she couldn't take it and run now. She needed to help these gryphons—and opinici.

She thought she smelled smoked meat up ahead, a rare eyrie delicacy, but as she came closer, she realized she was smelling a fire.

She stiffened. Around the corner, things were brighter. The padfeet had convinced an opinicus to light a stolen brazier. They were huddled around it for warmth.

Tielle frowned as she saw her one advantage slipping away in the bright light. Though the padfeet had their backs to the tunnel, she could see the faces of the hostages. Several peacock opinici and a half-dozen fantails were surrounded. While they'd all been harmed, none had been killed. The opinici cowered next to one of the water barrels.

"What are you going to do with us?" a fantail asked. His feathers were a mixture of brown and dark green with speckles of white on his tail. They'd separated him from the others.

This must be Golrin. It's too bad he doesn't know I'm coming or we could coordinate a plan.

"Nothing," a harpy gryphon said. "You tell us where the goldmint is, and we let you go. Simple. We're not bad gryphons. We just don't want to get sick."

"It's well-guarded," Golrin said. "It's located in the center of our nesting grounds. There are never fewer than a dozen guards."

The harpy laughed. "You're a liar, and while I love nothing more than a good story, a blizzard is coming."

"I'm not a liar," Golrin began, but a shadowy figure stepped into the light. It was one of the fantails Tielle had patched up, the one whose injuries were much lighter than the others.

"I already told them everything," the fantail traitor said. Tielle expected Golrin to look defeated.

Instead, he looked defiant. "Then you told them it was just an old medicine gryphon stash we found."

"I tasted some while you were trading," the traitor said. "They weren't dry. They were fresh and juicy. You lied to your pridemates the same way you're lying now."

Golrin didn't respond.

"Did you find the taiga gryphon?" the harpy eagle asked.

"No," the traitor replied. "She went off in the right direction but must have been fooled by the river. Taiga gryphons have always been dumb, but Williwaw are dimmest of them. She's probably given up and gone home."

Tielle's tail twitched in annoyance. Everyone knew the Snowfeather gryphons were the dumb ones.

Golrin perked up when he heard the taiga pride. He seemed to be looking past the fantails and padfeet. She took a gamble and stuck her head out so the light caught her blue eyes.

He bowed his head. Then he pretended to cough, stepping back towards the opinicus captives. He collapsed, nearly knocking over the water. One opinicus backed away, but the other helped him up. He whispered something to her, and she nodded.

Tielle wasn't sure what was going to happen next but had given up on calming her tail. It swayed back and forth in anticipation.

"Okay, I'll tell you," he said. "It's not far from here. I just ask that you give me a little now so I don't die from the cough before we arrive. When we get there, you'll have more than enough goldmint for all of you."

The harpy and fantail shared a look. Then one of the padfeet went to fetch a leaf wrap full of mint. As they offered it to Golrin, he began to cough, and with an exaggerated swipe, he knocked the mint into the brazier.

In an instant, five things happened.

A padfoot reached into the fire, burning his paws.

Golrin winked at Tielle.

The two opinici, pretending to help, poured the barrel of water onto the fire.

The fire went out, collapsing the cave into darkness.

The prisoners rushed out towards the tunnel to try to escape, grabbing random valuables on their way out.

Now, Tielle had her advantage again. She whispered to Golrin as he passed. "Follow the left side of the cavern. There are boxes halfway down."

Without an opinicus to strike a flint and tinder, the padfeet were struggling to stop their prisoners from escaping.

Tielle slipped between them, helping free fantails and opinici and pushing padfeet against each other to start conflicts between them.

Once the last of the prisoners had escaped, she knocked a few boxes over in the tunnel to help aid their escape and fled into the frigid, evening air.

In the darkness of the cave, Cici screamed for help. The cries of monitors unlike any Tielle knew of filled the hot, wet cave. The sounds were coming from between her and her brother. She took a step forward, but her entire body was poised to flee.

Short gasps of air left her lightheaded.

"I'll be fine!" Cici shouted. "You need to get out of the cave. One is coming straight towards you!"

She couldn't move. She could hear the lie in his voice.

She took a step towards him. She thought she heard something crunch and prayed it was a monitor.

She lifted her paw to take another step.

Her brother cried out in pain.

She pulled the paw back.

A single, heavy drop of water fell from above and landed on top of Tielle's beak.

She turned and fled back the way they'd come, through the darkness, and left her brother alone with the giant reptiles.

"Who are you?" Golrin demanded once they'd left the cave and flown into the relative safety of the fantail hunting grounds.

Li-Enn reunited with the other opinici. She was shivering, but they offered her their body heat as they looked through the things they'd stolen from the thieves' crates on the way out.

The last of the day's light had departed while they were in the cave, leaving them with the stars for illumination.

Stars that were quickly being swallowed up by clouds.

"Tielle of Williwaw," she said. "I came looking for goldmint to save my pride and found your comrades instead. The same mint you threw into the fire."

He didn't respond.

"I'll escort you south," she continued, "but I need to return home. The storm is coming, and I need to be with my pride."

"It's not just a storm," Li-Enn said. "It's an apocalypse. First the black ash, then the cold temperatures, and now a blizzard that crawls across mountains, scouring away life."

"Connixation." Tielle had never spoken the word in front of a stranger before. Storytellers had two types of tales they'd tell. The first were about the past, about the struggles gryphons had overcome. They were meant to inspire gryphons to become heroes, to work together, to be better.

But there was another type of tale, too. These were stories of the future. They weren't meant to inspire. They were warnings—with one storm, you could be erased from history.

Everyone was staring at Tielle. "It's the taiga version of the apocalypse. The entire world becomes ice, and we all die. That's the word our storytellers use: Connixation, the blizzard to end all life."

Li-Enn, on her back paws to take the weight off of her broken foreleg, nuzzled Golrin. "Give her the goldmint. Her pride needs it."

He sniffed. "Her pride is about to be wiped off the face of the weald by the apocalypse, didn't you hear her?"

"The goldmint was thrown into the fire," Tielle protested, but here, Golrin grinned.

He held out his paw. When he splayed the pads on his feet, there was goldmint stuck between each of them. It smelled, well, like feet—but that wouldn't inhibit its medicinal properties.

"They don't call me Golrin Goldpaw for nothing," he said with a bow.

Li-Enn pulled it from between his toes and stuffed it in Tielle's harness. "Don't let him fool you; they don't call him Golrin Goldpaw at all."

The taiga gryphon looked back and forth between the fantail and the opinicus. "So when you said join the fisherfolk, you really meant... join the fisherfolk?"

Golrin laughed, a short sound more like a guffaw, and put a wing over Li-Enn. "We'll see if the existing settlements will take us. If not, maybe we'll find an island and start our own."

"Get back to your pride," Li-Enn commanded Tielle. "There isn't much time. The storm will be past the eyrie by now."

Tielle started to leave, but Golrin grabbed her harness in his paw.

"You should take your entire pride and flee," he said. "You haven't heard the stories Li-Enn has been getting from the northern eyries. What's the word you used? Connixation? That's what's happening here."

You need to get out. It's coming straight towards you!

Cici's words echoed in Tielle's head. "I can't run from my problems. Besides, many of us are too sick to fly. Others are too stubborn. If it gets bad, we can always go stay at Hoarfrost."

Something inside of her screamed for her to flee with these fisherfolk aspirants. It took all of her willpower to speak the words of her pride leader and not what she truly thought.

Li-Enn looked at Tielle with pity. "Most of the eyries in the valleys survived. But the few in the mountains? They're gone. Nothing but ice and bodies remain. I know this'll sound like opinicus arrogance, but we built our spires to survive anything. What hope do a couple of gryphons in a cave have?"

"Directly south of the taiga is an island," Golrin continued. "It's a day and a half trip. That's our first stop. You wanted to know where the goldmint is from? Well, I've been picking it from islands off the coast. We're headed to the largest one first —it's just fields of goldmint and a pond. If we can't find shelter among the fisherfolk there, we'll keep going south."

Tielle took the goldmint but left their warnings behind.

Just as she was about to take flight, Li-Enn called after her, "When Hoarfrost is frozen solid, you're going to have to make a choice."

But the Williwaw gryphon's decision had been made for her when she left Cici behind. She wouldn't run away. Not now, not ever. She flew as fast as her dirty wings would let her.

WITH THE HELP of the kjarr pride, Tielle watched as they cleared the monitors out of the cave. Long, webbed spines flowed from the nape of their neck and down their backs. The kjarr gryphons called them sailfins.

With the help of a keen-sighted owl gryphon, they searched the cave. There was no sign of Cici. If he'd escaped, there was no evidence of it.

Tielle's parents stood behind her. Relief that their daughter had survived was overshadowed by their son's absence.

Her mother turned to the bodies of the sailfins. "Cut them open."

Tielle looked away while the owl gryphon cut open the sailfins' stomachs. There were some patches of white fur but not enough of a body to make an identification.

She moved a little way away from the cave entrance. She couldn't stand to be so close to the darkness. She kept thinking Cici would step out of the cave at any moment.

"She's only alive because she ran," Tielle's father said.

"Cici is only dead because she ran," her mother countered.

While her parents argued, Williwaw's pride leader walked up to Tielle. "Are you okay?"

She looked down at her paws. The warm spring felt cold. She shivered.

The pride leader groomed some of her matted fur.

"Will I be kicked out of the pride?" she asked.

"No, of course not." He lifted her face up and looked her in the eye. "But Tielle, you can't run from your problems. You have to promise me that."

She nodded. Her parents might never speak to her after today, but she'd be a good taiga gryphon. She'd never run again.

WILLIWAW'S MEDICINE gryphon prepared the goldmint into a paste for the sick.

"You couldn't get any more than this?" the pride leader asked Tielle. His feathers were frayed along the edges, and there were wrinkles around his eyes. The years since Cici's death had been hard on him.

She explained about Golrin Goldpaw, the fantail traders,

the harpy eagle padfeet, the peacock opinici, and the fisher-folk for the fifth time. Her pride seemed even less inclined to believe it now than they had been the first time she told them.

Cici had always loved her stories. Perhaps he was the only one. Or perhaps living through a real Connixation had ruined everyone's taste for tales of the end times.

Her parents were in the corner, coughing. The first mating season after their son's death, they'd refused to be near each other. The next year, what brought them together was their shared desire to avoid future loss. They never had another egg, but seeing them together kept other would-be suitors away.

Tielle's mother refused to look at her daughter even as she choked down the goldmint paste.

Everyone received a share of the medicine, and the effect was dramatic. Their voices cleared. The cough eased. Tielle felt hopeful for the first time in years.

"The first dose is what we call a false friend." The medicine gryphon settled in next to her. "Without more treatments, the cough will return in a few days. They look fine, even feel fine now, but it won't last."

Tielle frowned. "How long do they have?"

"Three days." The medicine gryphon kneaded more goldmint into a paste. "They'll fall sick again during the worst of the storm."

"Connixation," Tielle corrected.

A nearby fledgling whimpered.

The pride leader came over to scold her. "Don't use that word. You shouldn't have used it in front of the opinicus. They'll take it and strip it of meaning, use it for every small storm."

Her spine stiffened. "This isn't just any blizzard. Eyries

are gone. We're a small pride. We're going to get trapped in here."

Tielle's mother, reinvigorated by the elixir, stood. "Run if you're scared. No one here will stop you."

Cici had been Tielle's best friend, and her mom only gave voice to her own reservations.

The medicine gryphon finished divvying out the paste. "Everyone is well enough to fly a little way. We should go to Hoarfrost. I wouldn't say Connixation, but the signs are not good if we stay here. Ti said that Hoarfrost had been to the feathermane grounds to trade for goldmint. They won't turn us away. We're sister prides."

The pride leader looked from the medicine gryphon to Tielle's mother. "It would be warmer. Hoarfrost has space."

A sound like the kick of a goliath bird resounded throughout the small cave. Tielle jumped in spite of herself. More pounding came, along with shouts for help.

She rushed to the barrier. Heavy winds pushed from the other side. The barrier had been wedged shut against the storm, and it took the pride leader's help to get it open.

Several grey-furred gryphons spilled into the cavern.

"Matri?" Tielle asked. After Cici's death, she'd withdrawn into herself and lost track of her former friends.

"Why aren't you at Hoarfrost?" the pride leader said. "We're about to head there before the storm gets worse."

The two Hoarfrost gryphons ran to the fire to warm up.

With a chattering beak, Matri said, "It's too late. The barriers are all closed. They're frozen solid. We were out on patrol and couldn't get back in."

The Williwaw gryphons whispered among themselves.

"Why didn't you use the emergency exit?" Tielle asked. Every pride had a secret exit in case of an emergency from the days when opinici wouldn't tolerate gryphons within their borders. Hoarfrost's was on the weald side.

"Frozen all the way down," the second Hoarfrost gryphon managed. Her tail was more snow than fur.

"That's twenty gryphon lengths worth of ice." The pride leader's voice wasn't as certain as it had been moments before.

"Then we have no choice," Tielle's mother said. "We have to weather the storm here."

Tielle thought of Cici. She thought of the medicine gryphon's warning about the effects of the goldmint wearing off in three days. She thought about what would happen if the fire went out, if they were sealed inside.

"There's more mint on an island south of here, but it'll take all night and most of the next day to reach." She felt bad betraying Golrin's secret, but she wouldn't see her pride die if she could help it.

"We'd never make it back in time," Matri said. "We don't have an hour before the ice seals us in."

Tielle stood in front of the snow barrier. "You heard the medicine gryphon. We have three days. If you want to die cold and alone in the dark, you can stay here. If you want a chance at living, come with me. There's more goldmint. This is a slow-moving storm. We can reach Golrin's island and join the others. We stand a better chance if we're not trapped."

"Have you learned nothing? This is why Cici is dead." Tielle's mother spit on the ground.

Tielle bristled. "Cici's last words to me were that I had to flee. I shouldn't have left him behind. I'm sorry he's dead, but you don't have to die. You can fly away with me."

Internally, her heart warred with everything she'd been

told since Cici's death. She wanted to stay and be strong, but her desire to survive won out.

The two Hoarfrost gryphons removed themselves from the fire and stood next to Tielle. She nodded to Matri. Whatever they'd seen had convinced them.

The medicine gryphon joined them. "You'll need someone to turn the goldmint into paste."

"You promised you wouldn't run." The pride leader stood by Ti's mom.

Her father stood up. "She's only alive because she ran. I'm going with her."

Tielle's heart warmed, but she didn't wait to see who was moving towards the entrance. They didn't have time.

She pulled at the storm barrier with the help of the others. "It's time to go. Everyone knows Williwaw gryphons are the best mountain flyers. Let's live up to our reputation. Pretend the mountains continue into the water, and fly directly south until you see an island covered in goldmint."

She looked north to where Hoarfrost should be, but there was only a wall of white.

GOLRIN PULLED up as much goldmint as he could find while Li-Enn nursed her broken leg. Family and friends stood around eating and relaxing their wings. He'd been forced to leave several of his traders behind. The padfeet had left them with wing injuries. He prayed they would be okay. The other injured were doing the best they could.

When he'd last come here, the island had looked much larger. There'd been fields of gold surrounding a lake. Seeing it now, seeing how little cover there was, he felt less certain they would survive if the Connixation reached this far.

"You need to rest yourself, love," Li-Enn scolded him.

He shoved a pawful of goldmint into his harness. "We're going to have to head south. There's no place to weather the storm here."

"That's why you need to rest. How far to the next island?" She helped tie down the pouch on his harness.

"Half a day's flight." He stretched his long, fantail wings. The padfeet had bruised his tailfeathers. He should be grateful they didn't break his primaries, but the sea flight had been hard for him, and real worry began to creep in.

If Luminaire was frozen solid and this island was too small, his best hope lay on a mountain he'd once spotted even farther south. "Another half day after that to an island big enough to weather the storm on."

"We'll get there," Li-Enn said. "One island at a time. We'll stop, rest, and eat on each. There'll be opportunity enough to get some real sleep in once we're further from the storm."

"We should go now." Golrin didn't make any signs of getting airborne. He continued to watch the white sky.

Li-Enn groomed his neck ruff. "Your taiga rescuer will be fine. I'm sure the storm will die down before it reaches her mountain."

He looked north. The mainland had disappeared behind a wall of clouds. "You're a language scholar. What do you call that? The taiga gryphons would have a word for it."

"*Derecho*," Li-Enn said. "The Snowfeather word for that is a *derecho*. It's a mountain of living snow that feeds upon the unsuspecting."

He shivered. They hadn't come across any fisherfolk. The settlements on the shore had all been abandoned.

They'd all fled to...well, he hadn't the faintest idea where they'd fled to, but they weren't on the shore or Luminaire. He'd locate them later, once the weather cleared and the ash was gone.

A few snowflakes, pushed ahead of the rest by the winds, settled on his beak.

"It's time." He turned to go, but Li-Enn was watching some debris picked up by the storm. Grey shapes fluttered in the winds. One fell towards the water, barely righting herself before the waves took her.

"It's the taiga gryphons." Li-Enn said. They were headed off course. If they kept going in that direction, they'd pass the goldmint isle. It was hours to the next solid ground.

Li-Enn already had her flint and tinder fungus out and was trying to get a fired started. She had to use her good talons and her beak as her broken leg was still wrapped.

Golrin took to the air. The fantails who'd come with him, the ones who didn't trust the weald's trees to keep them safe, followed after.

He had to fly into Tielle to get her attention. "East! The first island is east."

The Williwaw Pride turned, but she stayed behind to make sure no one was left behind.

"How many of you are there?" He let the heavy winds push against his wings and tail, suspending him above the ocean.

"Twenty," she said. "The rest stayed behind."

He didn't ask how many *the rest* was. Instead, he sent his fantails to escort the taiga gryphons down to the first island.

"We didn't bring much food," Tielle shouted over the wind. "It didn't seem fair to those who stayed."

He guided her through the winds. "We have enough to share. This island is too small. Rest up, warm up, but when the storm arrives, we need to flee. There's a mountain in the ocean with cover against the storm, but it's another day's flight."

The taiga gryphons looked ready to collapse. Li-Enn had several fires going, and her opinicus family were unpacking food for the taiga gryphons along with another dose of gold-mint. Their large paws left ashen footprints all over the white stone of the island.

To the north, Luminaire disappeared beneath the derecho. He hoped the fisherfolk had made it okay.

He put a wing over Tielle to protect her from the wind. Li-Enn pulled out a device she called a brush to remove the ash from the taiga gryphon's coat without ingesting any of it.

He looked around. Opinicus, taiga gryphon, and fantail all helped each other recover.

"We found the fisherfolk after all," he mumbled.

Tielle looked around. "I don't see them?"

Li-Enn's eyes sparkled. "It's us. We're the fisherfolk— opinicus and gryphons working together."

He started to laugh but saw the ocean south of them starting to disappear. "Okay, we're out of time. One more island. Can you make it?"

Tielle nodded. "We have to."

"Iceberg!" Tielle called out, but she was wrong. She couldn't tell how long they'd been flying, but every part of her body ached. Even her mind had gone numb. Only once she'd said the words did she realize that she was seeing an actual mountain rising out of the ocean.

Her blue eyes searched for any sign of cover. A huge lake was frozen solid. The top of the mountain formed a caldera. If it had any caves, they were buried under ice and snow.

"There, on the west side," she pointed at a snowy outcropping that formed a right angle. "It looks like some sort of opinicus structure."

Golrin squinted. "I don't see it. It's all snow to me. How do we know it'll protect us?"

"I've seen a lot of snowy mountains in my time," she snapped back. "They don't look like that. There's a building or something buried there."

"We don't have time to argue." Li-Enn was losing altitude. "I can't fly any longer. I don't think the sick can, either. We have to make our stand here."

The first fantails and peacocks to land on the roof slid right off. The taiga gryphons' large paws gave them traction, and they all began to dig.

Matri was the first one to hit the wood underneath. "I found something! Wooden planks? Is this some sort of giant fisherfolk raft?"

Soon after, Tielle located a hole in the wood. The inside was a single large room full of snow, piles of broken lumber, and ice.

Tielle led the efforts to clear out the snow. The opinici began to light fires and search for more holes. Everything on the outside was already frozen solid, but there was no way to be sure what would happen when the Connixation hit. Some of the taiga gryphons explained how the snow barriers back home worked, and the opinici got to work creating them as best they could.

Golrin watched the north while the other fantails spread out and looked for signs of gryphons or opinici on the island. However long the wreckage had been here, its owners were long gone. There were a couple of smaller rafts, smashed to pieces, with a six-winged emblem on the sides, and the fantails did find signs of wildlife—both goliath birds and frost chickens—though Tielle wasn't sure they'd survive what was coming.

To the north, the ocean began to disappear. She redoubled her snow-clearing efforts until Li-Enn called for a halt.

"We need to seal the last snow barrier," the peafowl opinicus said. "It'll take time to freeze into place."

Tielle and her father used their blue eyes to search out any remaining fantail scouts, then she flew up to tell Golrin to come inside.

"It's time." She had to nudge him to get him to follow her back inside.

"Li-Enn said the Snowfeather Pride call it a *derecho*," he said. "A mountain of snow that hunts."

"A little poetic," Tielle mused. That did sound like how a taiga gryphon would explain it to an outsider. "It's more like anytime the clouds appear in a wall like that."

They were both mesmerized by how the storm seemed to swallow the ocean as it approached them.

"Do you think anyone survived?" he asked.

"I don't know. In the old stories, no one did." She led him down into the hold of the ship.

As Li-Enn sealed up the hole in the shipwreck, Tielle thought back to the types of stories medicine gryphons told: the types about the end of the world and the types that encouraged pride members to work harder and be better.

The medicine gryphon was busy tending to the sick. Overexertion had lessened the effect of the goldmint paste. Or had they flown for three days? It seemed impossible, but the winds had slowed them down. They'd had to land on several real icebergs halfway here. It was a miracle they'd only lost two—the female Hoarfrost gryphon and the

Williwaw pride leader who tried to pull her out of the water.

The oceans will freeze. The mountains will become tombs. There will be no more heat, no more life.

The Connixation, the end of the world. It was an old story. It had been Cici's favorite. They'd both stayed up late listening to the medicine gryphons talk about the apocalypse. When he couldn't sleep, he'd insist Tielle tell him the story as best she could from memory.

But there was more than one type of story.

Tielle stood up and addressed the assembled taiga gryphons, fantails, and opinici. The fisherfolk, as Golrin said. "Let me tell you the true story of the Connixation, and how the weald, eyrie, and taiga worked together to survive it..."

SILVER EYES

"There's been another outbreak." Deracho spread his wings to help shield his team from the wind. Several members were shivering, and while there were a few fellow taiga gryphons coming along for this mission, the bulk of his forces were Ashen Weald. Several rangers had been stationed nearby to guard the builders working on the path, and they'd offered their aid. The Ashen Weald was better equipped to deal with the infection, if not the snowstorm. He was grateful for their help.

He nodded to Thenca. She wore fur-lined armor designed by opinicus tailors and was flanked by two bog witches. While she'd gone back and forth from the taiga to the kjarr once a small path was made, Deracho's arrival in Snowfall had brought her back to the icy mountains to see him.

As long as he was in charge of Hoarfrost, they weren't able to spend any time together. She couldn't cross south of Glacial Run because of the wingtorns' pact with the fisher-folk. For the first time in years, they'd had an opportunity to have gryphlets together—right in time for him to be sent south. Now they struggled to find more than a few minutes in each other's company. Not that their current mission would afford them that opportunity.

The bog witches Thenca was mentoring were too inexperienced to risk in combat. They were younger than they first appeared. Once the infected were killed, however, they'd be in charge of burning the bodies. Their natural immunity to the parasite made them a necessity—they wouldn't become sick by handling the dead. The weald medicine gryphons had told them what precautions they needed to take so they didn't accidentally spread the infection to the rest of the team.

Several opinicus rangers shivered in the back. They tucked their long, blue heron necks against their bodies. They'd started complaining back at Snowfall Mountain and hadn't let up since.

Deracho hooted to his taiga gryphon pridemates, and they surrounded the blue opinici to keep them warm. "This is the resistant strain, but I don't want any of you to worry. We brought more than enough pumpkin to take care of all of us, should it come to that."

"I thought the resistant strain was only in the south, around Sandpiper's Dune and Hoarfrost," the male bog witch said. "Do we know how it got up here?"

The bog witches were all stolen eggs. They'd been raised as gryphlets without parents or a den mother, and their social niceties around other prides were still a little lacking. They could be a bit blunt at times.

"It's not clear." Deracho had his suspicions. One of the scouts who survived the initial starling attack on Hoarfrost, a snowy owl gryphon named Lenti, had gone missing. Over the last few months, the medicine gryphons had been treating him for the resistant strain. He'd fluctuated between recovering and getting worse up until a week ago, when he'd disappeared. Yesterday, one of the gryphons Biski assigned to check the taiga wildlife caught signs of an outbreak where he'd last been seen.

"There's at least one scout missing," Thenca said. As the only wingtorn, getting her out here had been a logistical nightmare, but her familiarity with the taiga made her the natural choice to lead the Ashen Weald side of the joint operation. "That's why we're grateful for the rangers' help. We'd like to capture him alive if he's infected. We'll burn the wildlife. There isn't enough pumpkin to make curing them reasonable at this point."

She went through several safety precautions. After New Eyrie and the stories from the bog expedition, they all had a good idea of what to expect from the infected. Nobody liked to be near them, but everyone here was a volunteer, even the grouchy rangers.

The storm howled, and Thenca shivered. "I know the snow and winds aren't ideal, and they're only going to get worse over the next few days. That's just what winter is like in the taiga. This is probably our best opportunity to stop the spread."

"Thenca and our bog friends will set up camp in the cave over there." Deracho belatedly realized that they could be having this conversation inside the cave, but it was a good opportunity to help their Ashen Weald friends build character. "Once the rangers get a fire going and a snow barrier up, they'll wait at the entrance while the taiga pride locate wildlife and, hopefully, our missing scout. Then it's their turn."

One of the rangers, a captain, stretched out his long, blue heron neck. "The taiga gryphons will take care of any frost chickens or small birds they find. If they see a goliath, they'll send one gryphon to fetch us while another flies above the bird to mark its location. And if anyone locates the scout, it'll be up to all of us working together to subdue him safely."

The other rangers didn't complain, either because the captain outranked them or because their beaks had frozen shut. Deracho made a cooing sound, and the blue-eyed taiga gryphons headed into the snow-covered aneda forest to begin searching. With any luck, they'd finish before the snowstorm forced them to stay the night.

ONCE THE RANGER'S fire was in full swing, Thenca knew how to keep it burning. The opinici set up a barrier of pelts to keep the worst of the wind and snow out of the cave, then settled in to wait for word.

Thenca conversed with the bog witches. Bringing them along on this excursion provided her with an opportunity to help teach them what it meant to be a part of the Ashen Weald. The male asked a lot of questions about what the bog pride was like before he was born. She did her best to answer them, but she'd been a gryphlet back then.

She'd assumed the other bog gryphon was just quiet, but when the male ran off to ask the rangers some questions, his associate finally opened up to Thenca.

"Are you my mother?" the bog witch asked.

"No." This was not a question Thenca was prepared for, but she definitely knew the answer. "What's your name?"

"My friends call me Petal." Her nares blushed with embarrassment. "I didn't mean to insult you. It's just that we look a lot alike."

Thenca would have to take her word for it since it was

impossible to tell what Petal looked like under all of that blue paint. While her face and undersides were covered with skeletal patterns, the tops of her wings had been painted to look like aneda needles.

"Gryphons don't always look like their parents," Thenca explained, "and I didn't have an egg before we were captured, so I think it's safe to say I'm not your mother."

Petal sat in silence.

"Are a lot of the bog witches looking for their parents?" Thenca asked.

Petal nodded.

"I don't think there's any way for them to find out, not for certain," Thenca said. It'd been two and a half years since the bog witches had all been stolen and raised in a sunken eyrie. Since their recent reunion with the remains of the wingtorn, there'd been relief but also confusion. Many of them had been kjarr eggs, and none of them knew who their parents were. Before they'd even hatched, they'd been taken first by the rangers, and then by a rogue faction of bog gryphons, most of whom were now dead.

Petal fidgeted, and Thenca was still searching for some words of kindness when the first of the taiga scouts came through the pelts and into the cave.

"We found some gryphon tracks nearby, on the other side of the mountain." The taiga gryphon's eyes were so blue they glowed in the firelight. "Deracho's following them, but he wants all the rangers to come out and be ready with their nets."

The taiga gryphons and rangers left, leaving Thenca alone with Petal and the other bog witch to tend the fire. Thenca didn't know any more tales from the bog, so she started telling them about her and her brother's adventures with the Ashen Weald.

"The walls of New Eyrie were lined with spikes, and the sky was full of opinici. There was a horde of infected starlings to the south, but Urious didn't know that yet..."

Deracho used his wings to shield his face against the winds. When he'd put together this mission, he'd been worried he wouldn't find any trace of Lenti. Instead, he was actually finding too much evidence.

Tracks went off in all directions. Over the last week, the infected scout had walked all over the mountain. Snow slides had covered some tracks, winds had obscured others, and Deracho was having a hard time finding anything fresh. He worried that meant the gryphon had either frozen to death or left the area. Neither were outcomes he wanted to consider. Not when Lenti had eggs back home that would hatch come spring.

Deracho followed a set of tracks south, taking care of a few frost chicken dens on his way, until they disappeared into a snowbank. There was a lump buried under a foot of snow.

Is this him? He began to dig.

"Please be okay in there, friend," Deracho whispered. He made it through the snow and his paws touched wet feathers. He left his foreleg there for a moment and thought he could detect a slight heartbeat.

His hopes rose until he burrowed a little further and got a glimpse of grey. The mound of snow began to shake, and a feral goliath bird freed itself with an angry *Mronk!*

Instinct took over, and Deracho jumped straight up to escape.

His heart leapt into his stomach as the goliath got the

better of him. It pulled him out of the air and slammed him into the ground.

The snow crunched beneath his fall. The air was knocked out of him. His head spun. He shouted for help with a touch of panic in his voice. He'd been so worried about finding Lenti, he let his guard down.

The goliath's eyes didn't have a silver sheen, but that didn't mean it wasn't in the early days of infection. The silver took a while to set in, and a healthy goliath was just as deadly as an infected one.

Deracho stood up on his back paws and spread his wings as wide as they would go. It was common knowledge that if you ran from one of these birds, they knew you were prey. Instead, he backed up slowly towards the woods. If he could get an aneda tree between him and his opponent, he could buy himself enough time to get airborne.

"Mronk!" the bird repeated. It crouched down, bringing it to eye level with Deracho. Closer to Hoarfrost, the feral goliaths could reach fifteen feet tall. This one was still growing and stood only three feet higher than a gryphon.

He had to lower himself to all fours to back up farther, but he kept his wings out wide and his tail straight up. He waved it a bit. With any luck, the goliath would attack the black spot on the tip before it attacked him. At least, he hoped that wasn't an old medicine gryphon tale. This would be his first time putting it to the test. Normally, he was smart enough not to fight goliaths on the ground.

Luck was on his side. Several taiga gryphons and rangers appeared in the sky above him, but the goliath bird looked about ready to take a bite out of him just to sate its curiosity.

Deracho rose up again on two legs to look more intimidating. It was working until he took a step. His foot caught in a hole in the snow, and he fell onto his back, twisting his paw.

The goliath bird charged him, biting down to try to catch his throat. Deracho rolled out of the way, but the bird caught his hip in its beak.

He stuck all four sets of claws into its face and pushed off. The bird screeched and fell backwards.

Deracho leapt onto his paws and groomed his side and hip to see how the damage was. To his surprise and relief, the goliath had come away with a beakful of fur and no flesh.

Thenca would have killed me if that bird had bitten anything important. He considered what she'd say when she found out that he'd dug a goliath out of its burrow instead of letting the rangers handle it. *She may still kill me yet.*

The goliath regained its footing. It shook its head, splattering the snowy hillside with drops of blood. He'd missed its eyes and made it mad.

The bird reared up and tried to stomp on Deracho, but by then, his mind had found its hunting calm. He slipped to the side. When the bird's massive foot landed, becoming lodged in the same snow he'd tripped over, he leapt up and caught its neck with his beak.

Its heavy, fur-like feathers and thick hide kept it safe. It shook him off the same way it had the blood. Just when it turned to stomp again, one of the ranger's nets enveloped it and brought it down. Another ranger with jelly toxin arrived to render it unconscious while they killed it and prepared to burn the body.

"Are you okay?" The ranger captain was looking at his waist, where there was a huge clump of missing fur. "Let's get a dose of pumpkin into you."

Deracho accepted the orange vial, letting the ranger pull

out the stopper. No one knew how cooking the pumpkin or adding spices would affect its medicinal properties, so for the moment, everyone was drinking it raw in an alcohol-based tincture.

Deracho coughed once but didn't spit it back up. "I was looking for the missing scout, but I found a goliath bird instead."

"This area seems to be full of them," the captain said. "Your pridemates flagged around a dozen. We have our work cut out for us. I hear this is called Goliath Mountain? It's well-named."

"If the scout is infected and we don't find him, this'll just start anew." Deracho didn't confirm the mountain's name. One of the games they played with the weald and kjarr gryphons was making up names for different mountains. In truth, the only mountains that had names were the ones where prides had lived: Hoarfrost, Williwaw, Snowfall, and Snowfeather.

He looked down at his twisted back paw. It hurt but not enough for him to head back and give up looking for his friend. He searched for what he'd tripped over. Frost chickens built dens under the snow. It would be safer to kill and burn them now if that's what he'd stumbled over.

He followed the burrow back another ten feet. Before he located the chickens, however, he stumbled across fresh gryphon tracks headed back towards the mountain. Lenti still lived.

"There are some chickens here that need to be taken care of," he told a nearby ranger. "I'm going to stop in at the base camp and get some ointment for the scratches. Tell your captain we should finish checking this area in another couple of hours, then we can head back to Snowfall and get something to eat, assuming the weather holds."

The ranger saluted and flew off. By the way the snow was starting to come down, the weather wouldn't hold.

THENCA WAS JUST TELLING the bog witches about her various mountain-climbing efforts when the makeshift snow barrier was pulled up and a ranger came in, leaving it open behind her.

"What news of the storm?" Thenca asked. "Need our help yet?"

The ranger nodded. "We've killed a dozen goliaths now. At least a couple were showing signs. Deracho himself decided to go paw-to-claw with one on the ground. I think he's coming to get patched up, but after that, it's about time to move the bodies into the other cave and get a pyre going. I'll leave that to you and the other immune."

The bog witches looked relieved that they wouldn't have to kill the goliath birds themselves. They went through their supplies. Most of their treatments involved pastes made from flowers or fish of different sorts, but the local medicine gryphons had given them pumpkin and aneda poultices, too.

Thenca was about to tell the ranger to close the snow barrier when her eyes rested on a familiar sight: the outline of a snowy owl gryphon. Deracho was making his way towards the cave from around twenty feet out.

She watched him run closer, wondering why he hadn't landed by the entrance. Her hackle feathers rose. He never had that effect on her. She looked into his eyes to see what was wrong, but the eyes that looked back at her weren't blue.

They were silver.

This wasn't Deracho. It was the missing taiga gryphon.

"Close the barrier!" she shouted to the ranger, but it was too late. The infected scout crashed through it, smashing the opinicus against the cave wall. It chomped down on her with its beak.

"Behind the fire!" Thenca pushed the bog witches. Then she charged into the infected taiga gryphon, sending them both sprawling out into the snow.

They went tail-over-beak down the mountain in a tangle. Just when she thought she'd found purchase under the layer of snow, she came away with a pawful of scree and roots. They finally crashed twenty feet down into a small crevasse.

Luckily for her, the infected gryphon took the brunt of the fall. Its wings must have broken, but it didn't show any indication it was in pain. It bit at Thenca but was rebuffed by her leather armor.

She shouted, letting the stone on either side of her amplify her voice. No response came, but there was a slight tremor on the ledge above them. She cried out a second time, but the tremor grew, and she feared an avalanche.

The infected bit and clawed at her. She resisted the urge to kill it and instead worked to create some distance between them. Lenti had a family back at Snowfall. While Deracho hadn't mentioned it to prevent putting the team in unnecessary danger, she knew he was hoping to save this gryphon.

The snowstorm's intensity grew. She cried out a third time, and instead of a ranger or taiga scout, the two bog witches looked down over the ledge at her.

Great, she thought. *I end up with the only two bog witches who don't have experience hunting the infected.*

The scout attacked again, and this time it managed to get its claws through her armor.

She yelped in pain, then shouted up at the young gryphons. "Fetch Deracho or the captain!"

The male bog witch disappeared, but Petal tried to fly down. She made it partway when a gust of wind slammed her against the rock face. She tumbled into the crevasse behind the infected.

At the young witch's cry, the infected turned towards the sound. He stalked towards her, his large paws finding purchase atop the snow.

While Petal screamed in terror, and Thenca found something rocky to push off from. She leapt onto the scout's back. If it came down to the taiga gryphon or Petal, Thenca would choose the uninfected every time. There was no guarantee that they'd be able to bring him back.

The scout shook Thenca off, sending her flying with pawfuls of shed fur. In a last ditch attempt to draw him away from Petal, Thenca used her mockingbird talents to roar at it in Jun the Kjarr's loudest voice.

This time, the snow on the ledge above didn't just rumble, it collapsed into the crevasse, burying all three gryphons.

DERACHO ARRIVED at the cave and found a wounded ranger and a trail of displaced snow leading down the mountain. The opinicus had a nasty bite taken out of her, but an aneda poultice was holding the important bits in, at least for now. Before she could tell him what was going on, one of the bog witches showed up.

"Deracho!" the male witch said. "Thenca's with an

infected gryphon in a canyon. Petal fell in after them. They need your help."

Deracho didn't waste any time. "Go fetch the ranger captain. I'll help Thenca and Petal."

He ignored the heavy winds and followed the trail. If Thenca had gone over the edge, he didn't know what he'd do. Younce, the new taiga pride leader, had warned Deracho this would be a difficult section of the taiga for her to reach by paw, but he hadn't listened. Instead, he'd let his desire to spend time with her override any safety concerns.

The trail went over the edge and into a crevasse full of snow. His first thought was that they must have rolled past it. He began to fly by when he noticed that the trail didn't continue on the other side. There was also a sound coming from beneath the ground.

His owl-like hearing caught the sound of scratching and shuffling under him. He burrowed into the ground, trying to track the sound through the snow. He extended his claws to try to displace the snow faster. His claws went into her beak, but he didn't have time to apologize.

"Petal's also buried," Thenca's scratched beak said. "I have my armor. She's not wearing anything. She'll freeze if you don't get her out."

He assumed Petal was the other bog witch. He hadn't learned their names yet. All sorts of Ashen Weald came and went in the taiga as construction on the path progressed. Gryphons with skull face paint weren't any stranger than the fantails with their long, feathered tails or the parrotfaces who insisted on walking everywhere.

He thought he heard sounds coming from a few feet away, so he began to dig again. This time, the beak he unearthed tried to bite him. It was Lenti.

He grabbed a branch off an aneda tree growing out of

the rock face and stuffed it in his friend's mouth. While Lenti chewed on the bitter bark, he dug where the snow was lumpy.

The infected thrashed around, but with its wings buried under the avalanche, it was having trouble making any headway. Thenca, meanwhile, used her beak to free one of her paws and was nearly above the snow. She shivered.

Deracho located a third gryphon under the snow. This time, he remembered to retract his claws. "Can you hear me? Are you okay?"

"It was so c-c-c-old," Petal stuttered, "but now I feel like my paws are on fire."

Deracho frowned. There was a point where the feeling of cold was replaced by heat. What came next was frostbite —and worse.

He redoubled his efforts until a loud hiss come from behind him.

"Stay with it," Thenca shouted. "I'm just about free. I'll keep Lenti off you."

The hissing grew louder.

THENCA LIBERATED her second forepaw and started to wriggle free. Her brother had teased her mercilessly about the warm armor, but he wasn't spending half of his time in the mountains. The warmth had kept her from going into shock, and she was grateful, but she had some ideas about improvements that could be made in the future, especially around the paws.

The infected scout shook his entire body, dislodging the last of the snow entombing him. Whether this was a primal instinct or something taiga gryphons were taught, she didn't know. He pulled himself up with a loud hiss.

"Stay with it," she shouted to Deracho. "I'm just about free. I'll keep Lenti off you."

"She says her paws feel hot," he shouted back.

Thenca knew what that meant. They didn't have much time.

She pulled her back legs out of the snow and shook as hard as she could. She didn't give Lenti an opportunity to go for her mate. While his attention was on Deracho, she leapt on top of the infected scout. He rolled onto his back to bite and scratch at her, but her armor took the worst of it. She pinned him against the rock face.

"Got her!" Deracho freed Petal from the snow. She was limp. He tried to get airborne, but her fur and feathers were soaked through, and she weighed too much. He started dragging her towards the side of the crevasse and up to the surface.

Thenca cried out when one of the scout's claws pierced her armor.

Deracho started to come back for her.

"Don't stop!" she shouted. "Get Petal to warmth. I can hold him here."

More claws found purchase, and she stifled a scream.

"Where are the rangers?" Deracho's words were barely audible over the snowstorm. He hesitated, unable to leave her, but unable to do anything about it. Finally he extended his claws and came towards the scout. There was a determination in his blue eyes that she didn't like the look of.

"Don't do it!" she shouted. "I'll be okay. We'll cure him. Just get Petal to safety."

He pulled back his paw but couldn't bring himself to finish Lenti. Deracho raised and lowered his claws several times, and just when he looked determined enough to do it, a haunting heron cry came from overhead. The ranger captain landed.

A dose of jelly toxin finally rendered the scout limp. With the arrival of the rest of the rangers and the taiga gryphons, they were able to use their largest net to transport Petal to the cave before they returned for the infected taiga gryphon.

With some assistance, Thenca got her paws back on solid ground. She hurt all over, and her armor was shredded. By the time she reached the cave, they had another problem.

"The storm is getting worse," the captain said. "If you want us to airlift one of you out of here, now's the time."

He looked at Petal, Thenca, the chomped ranger, and the infected scout in turn. The ranger's wounds had been tended to enough to let her fly.

"Take Lenti to the medicine gryphons first," Thenca said. "We'll keep Petal warm here and help raise her temperature. If the storm obliges, come back for her."

"What about you?" The male bog witch looked at her lack of wings. "You don't want to get trapped here, do you?"

Thenca shook her head. "I'm happy enough staying here by the fire with Deracho until we get a break in the weather."

The rangers were unsure, but a taiga gryphon came in to say that the storm was getting worse by the minute. They wrapped the lost scout in a net, secured the snow barrier as best they could, and vanished into the snowy sky, weighed down by their cargo. The taiga gryphons also departed, leaving Thenca and Deracho alone with the two bog witches. They'd refused to be separated.

There were several pelts left over from the barrier, which

Thenca turned into a burrow for Petal and the others. Deracho lent his warmth to the endeavor, and every so often, the male bog witch checked Petal and Thenca's wounds and gave Deracho another vial of pumpkin to drink.

Once Petal was warm enough to be out of danger, he relaxed a little but also sighed. "She really thought you were her mother. She seemed sure of it."

Thenca opened a sleepy eye. "I already told her it couldn't be true. I never had any children."

It was always possible Petal was one of Urious's offspring. Thenca had never come out and asked her brother directly. Instead, she'd just assumed he'd spent every mating season pining over Ari, who'd only had eyes for Jun back then.

"You seem old," the young bog witch said. "Did you just not want gryphlets?"

Deracho puffed up, but Thenca put a paw on his beak to settle him down.

"I suppose I feel old after all that's happened," she said. "In the time since I met Deracho, generations have gone by. First, Mignet and Satra grew up. Then half of the next hatch year was kept in cages. You were the other half, still eggs, who hatched soon after. We were dosed with red fern in captivity, so you were the last batch. Until spring comes, you're the youngest gryphons in our pride."

"Isn't the kjarr den mother taking care of you?" Deracho asked. "You're only just adults."

The male bog witch considered his next words. "The kjarr pride is more concerned about the children they know are theirs. They're not really sure what to do with us."

Thenca and Deracho shared a look. There was enough

of a history between them that she already knew what he was thinking.

"You're needed at Hoarfrost," she told him. "Another few years and you could be made pride leader of the first new taiga pride since the Connixation."

"Why would I want to be leader of a pride situated where you can't go?" There was a sparkle in his eye. "We've talked about having an egg together, opinicus-style. Why don't we go help the lost-and-found bog gryphons?"

Curled up by the fire, Petal opened an eye.

"They're not gryphlets." Thenca turned to the male bog witch. "No offense intended. But you're adults, even if just. You don't really need a den mother."

There was a time in her life when being a den mother was inconceivable to her, but after all that had happened, she was starting to reconsider. She'd basically raised Satra already, and she spent a good deal of her time at Snowfall playing with the gryphlets.

More than that, there was something honest and refreshing about being away from the politics and horrors of the last three years. She wanted this to be a time of rebuilding, and part of that was raising the next generation to make sure they didn't repeat their parents' mistakes. This was something she could do that would make a real difference.

But this wouldn't be a conventional den mother role. Unlike the hostage gryphlets who had taken an extra year to fledge because of malnutrition, the gryphons hatched from the stolen eggs had matured at their normal rate. The things they had seen and done in the bog had the unintentional effect of making them seem older than the other half of their hatch-year who'd been kidnapped to the Redwood Valley.

"We need something," the male bog witch said. "Just

someone to ask questions of. Maybe not a den mother, but the world is different from how we were taught. When we realized we weren't going to find our parents, many of us retreated back to the new settlement, Bogwash. I worry that if we don't do something, many of us are going to turn feral again."

Thenca was thinking it through. Deracho, showing uncharacteristic wisdom, kept his beak shut. She looked from Petal to the other bog witch. She and Deracho were only just now considering if they wanted gryphlets. And, if they did, whether they'd be handing them off to the taiga den mother or trying to raise them like opinici might.

The Ashen Weald's new Crackling Sea opinicus members had started to normalize mating for life even among its gryphon members. While the fisherfolk had always been like that, she'd been barred from coming anywhere near the shore, which limited their options. In the last few months, many Ashen Weald gryphon couples decided they wanted recognition of their bond, opening an opportunity for Deracho when they ultimately made that decision.

But there was a lot she still didn't know about raising offspring. Den mothers normally trained for years. This might be an opportunity to speed up her own learning by finding out what the recovered bog pride felt they still needed to learn.

"Okay," she said at last. "We'll go down to Bogwash. We'll answer everyone's questions about the world. We'll spend the spring there doing what we can. But *just* the spring. I'm not spending summer among the mangroves. I'm not grooming swamp gunk and sea salt out of your fur in the blistering heat. The moment the weather turns, we head home."

Next to her, still mostly buried in blankets, Petal smiled.

Thenca rolled her eyes and looked at Deracho's missing clump of fur. "You know, last time we were caught in a cave during a snowstorm, things were a lot more romantic."

This time, it was Deracho who put a paw over her beak. "Not in front of the gryphlets."

His blue eyes twinkled right before she hit him in the face.

BLUE-EYED FESTIVAL

WARNING: SPOILERS FOR STARLING

On the shortest day of the year, Snowfall Mountain was living up to its name. The beautiful rock formations and aneda forests of the taiga were covered in an ever-growing layer of thick snow. Atop the peak, snowy owl and gyrfalcon gryphons worked hard to clear their nesting grounds before the guests arrived. Several opinicus patrols struggled to secure a stormcloth roof atop the amphitheater where the celebration would take place after nightfall.

Not that dark was far away. The sun had long ago disappeared behind thick clouds.

Younce, leader of the taiga pride, finished clearing out the common area and went to find warmth. The dark rosettes in his fur were obscured by snow. Even the black bars on his wings were gone. Only his bright eyes stood out as he settled down around the fire to preen himself dry.

"I almost did not recognize you," Tresh said. The black and white petrel fisherfolk had come up early to help with preparations. Since the winter snowstorms had started in earnest, few had been willing to fly all the way up to Snowfall, herself included. Instead, Younce had made it a habit to check on the southernmost taiga pride outposts—the ones near where Tresh lived in particular.

"Oh?" he managed through a beakful of ice and fur.

She came over to help, starting with his fluffy tail. "I keep looking for green eyes."

All around the campfire, snowy gryphons with blue eyes were grooming themselves dry. In the summer, the pride's eye colors ranged from brown to orange to green. Only when the days became shorter in the autumn did their eye color change as the lens stretched to give them better night vision. Here at midwinter, every taiga gryphon shared the same eye color.

"What is it like?" she asked. While the fishing village where she'd grown up had gryphons and opinici of all sorts, the few taiga fisherfolk lived on an island several days flight from shore by themselves, only coming to the mainland to trade.

Younce licked a paw and groomed snow out of his ear. "The daylight becomes softer, fuzzier. It gets harder to see for long distances. But the darkness opens up. Every night, no matter how dark, looks as though the moon were full and bright."

Thenca, one of the wingtorn gryphons helping direct the stormcloth roofing efforts, padded over to join their conversation. She had on a fur-lined harness to help stay warm. "Some gryphons start to sleep during the day and only come out at night. Much to the chagrin of their loved ones who would like to spend the few daylight hours with them."

Across the common area, her snowy owl mate, Deracho, was just waking up and crawling out of his cave with a big yawn. He still had a large patch of fur missing from his hip after a run-in with an ornery goliath bird.

"Is Satra coming?" Younce asked Thenca. Satra the Kjarr now controlled the Ashen Weald, an alliance of gryphons and opinici unheard of in modern times. Managing an eyrie and seven prides was a large task for anyone. It was made more difficult by the fact that several of those prides had lost leaders.

Strix had died the night the Redwood Valley burned down. Zrim Feathermane had been killed by the swarm of infected starlings that nearly wiped out New Eyrie and the Ashen Weald at the same time. Erlock Fantail had disappeared into the Emerald Jungle, seeking to bring a cure to the starlings who had yet to become infected. The Crackling Sea Eyrie let the rangers, their military, rule over them after their previous leader had been killed by Blackwing assassins. And nearly a hundred gryphons, stolen as eggs, had returned to their birthplace as young adults—and bog witches. The prides remembered the lost as well as the newly found.

It would be reasonable for Satra to go back on her promise to come to the Blue-eyed Festival. Still, Younce held out hope. She'd never been given an opportunity to grieve. Nor, really, an opportunity to meet other gryphons who had loved Mignet. He hoped tonight would remedy that.

If the snow would let up.

"I don't know if *anyone* is going to be able to arrive." Thenca curled up with Deracho on one side and the fire on the other, filling in the gap in his fur with her body. "Who all did you invite? You're not going to get any wingtorn up the mountain in this weather."

Tresh shivered and pushed against Younce's warm coat. "He had me bring invitations to Zeph and Kia on Luminaire. And I left an invitation for the taiga islanders at Sandpiper's Dune."

"They fled the night of the Connixation and never came back," Younce explained. "Everyone they knew died in the Connixation, frozen as they slept. We buried their frozen ancestors as we dug out the old nests. I'm hoping that if family won't bring them back, maybe an opportunity to celebrate will."

"Sugar frogs," Deracho said sleepily. "If they decide to fly all the way up here, they'll do it just to find out what real sugar frogs taste like."

Thenca laughed. "They're sweet. And, if you don't eat them fast enough, they hop away. What more is there to know?"

"They've been gone for generations," he replied. "I'll bet they've heard stories. They'll be here; you'll see. What did Zeph and Kia say?"

"Zeph? Like the Reeve's Bane Zeph?" Thenca asked. "He's one of the copper hawks in Hatzel's pride, isn't he?"

Younce had sent an invitation to Hatzel, but she'd declined. After killing the previous taiga pride leader, her childhood friend and Mignet's father, she hadn't returned to the taiga. Younce had also attempted to send an invitation to Ninox, but her entire pride had disappeared overnight.

"Zeph grew up here," Younce explained. "He hatched the same year as me and Mignet. He only left to go south after he'd fledged."

The first of the guests were arriving, covered in snow and looking for food and warmth. Younce gave himself one last shake to make sure he was dry. He walked past several sculpted snow-gryphons, the products of youngsters bursting with energy for the festival. While Deracho had slept, Thenca helped the latest batch of gryphlets learn to make them with a little help from their opinicus friends.

They all had shiny stones for eyes and carved wood for beaks.

He went by a whole row of them. Unlike the taiga pride in winter, pretty rocks gave each snow-gryph a different set of colored eyes.

Only one snow-gryph had bright blue eyes. He stared at them for a few minutes. They looked familiar. He didn't know what stones were used, but the snow gryphon looked life-like. He could have sworn it had fish breath.

He shrugged and turned back in time to see a red, green, and blue shape descend on the northern edge of Snowfall. It had been months since he'd last seen her, but Kia's colorful plumage was hard to mistake. As she settled in alone, Younce was left to wonder where Zeph was. He never missed an opportunity for a free meal—or mischief.

Too late, Younce's brain finally realized why the eyes on the snow gryphon behind him looked so familiar.

Zeph burst out of his snowy hiding place, a twinkle in his bright blue eyes and the smell of fish on his breath, and pounced Younce with a laugh.

SATRA THE KJARR had never been a strong flyer. Two years under constant guard in an eyrie hadn't given her many opportunities to test her wings. Her jailors had become nervous if she approached the city limits, so she'd kept her time in the sky limited. Guilt, too, had kept her on the ground. At the time, she'd been the only adult gryphon of her pride whose wings hadn't been chopped off. She walked out of respect for their loss.

She often lamented not being better in the air. Between sea monsters, three eyries worth of conflicts, and starlings, she'd resolved to improve her skills. Unfortunately, a few months of training hadn't fixed years of atrophy, and nothing had prepared her for flying through a snowstorm.

She considered turning back twice. While the second time was snow-related, the first was when she flew over the frozen lake where Mignet had drowned. Satra was running late after dealing with parrotface drama and hadn't picked her route well.

Despite Younce's assurances that the Blue-eyed Festival was a time for remembrance, she remained unconvinced of the need. She'd never forgotten Mignet. The war and Satra's capture had happened soon after Mignet's death. She'd never forgotten Mignet because that was the last time she had been happy.

Just when the snowstorm was picking up and she was worried she'd gotten lost, Satra saw the edge of the path and landed at an outpost. It was abandoned—its inhabitants had gone to the weald or sea to spend the holiday with their families—but it gave her an opportunity to warm up before she went the rest of the way. Her paws and beak were chattering, and despite hours of practice, it took fifteen minutes for her to finally get the flint and tinder fungus going. She stayed only as long as it took to warm up and dry her feathers, then she continued on her way. If the taiga was cold and wet during the day, it would be worse once the sun went down.

She reached Snowfall after dark. With the path and mountain covered in snow, she almost flew past it. She was expecting to see fifty gryphons celebrating on top of a mountain. When she only saw snow, she assumed she'd missed it. Then she realized she was seeing a covering with firelight peeking out along the edges and remembered the ranger lord had gifted them a stormcloth roof—against the protestations of the opinici he ruled who considered the cloth sacred.

Satra landed just outside the covering and steeled herself. In private, she'd been able to mourn Mignet as best she could. But in public, Satra was the head of the Ashen Weald. It would be hard to reconcile those two parts of herself tonight. She'd have declined Younce's invitation, but he was right. As time went by, she'd begun to feel haunted by Mignet's memory. She didn't think this would help, but she was willing to give it a try. If nothing else, it would be nice to taste sugar frogs again.

ONCE YOUNCE and Zeph were done retelling each of their versions of the starling invasion of Hoarfrost, Younce excused himself to check on the other guests. Zeph was now talking about bringing bees from the weald down to the shore, which was a story that Younce didn't feel obligated to stick around and correct.

Despite the taiga pride leader's best efforts to keep the tale of Hoarfrost straight, someone had painted a picture of him on the walls in bright pink with silvery stains under his eyes. There were a few fledglings who had figured out a reasonable imitation of the dye recipe that had stained him in the first place and turned themselves pink, much to the annoyance of their parents—and the next set of gryphons to try to use those hot springs. Thankfully, Biski's miracle soap was something they'd stocked up on.

Younce chatted with the various guests. While the snowstorm had kept some of them away, there were still representatives from across the kjarr, bog, weald, and sea chatting and having a good time. He was glad. He heard several young taiga gryphons doing their best imitation of a purr as they tried to flirt. With such a small pride, all gryphlets came through liaisons with other prides. The Blue-eyed Festival offered most of them their first opportunity to get to know their weald friends.

Or opinicus friends, he amended. Two opinici were cooking salted meat over a brazier and offering it to the other guests. While salted goliath bird or capybara was a staple at lower elevations, it was a rarity atop Snowfall, and the opinici were getting a lot of taiga attention. The den mother might see some opinicus chicks mixed in with the taiga gryphlets come spring. They'd never been squeamish about that sort of thing at the higher altitudes. Even Mignet's mother had been an opinicus, albeit one who was now among those who'd gone missing in the bog.

Speaking of missing, other than Hatzel and the taiga islanders, only Satra was absent. A commotion near the edge of the amphitheater caught his eye, and he saw the golden crest of a kjarr gryphon and made his way over.

"If you're going to invite the other prides up here," the Kjarr said, "the least you can do is make sure it's warm and sunny."

"Oh, we hold that festival in the summer," he said. "It's called the No-longer-blue-eyed Festival. Sadly, the sugar frogs have all defrosted by then. Mostly, we sit around and complain about all the shedding."

Satra laughed, and Younce realized how nervous she must be coming up here. The last time she was surrounded by this many taiga gryphons, Mignet lay dead at her feet, and they were demanding to take her into custody. Only Thenca's timely arrival had let Satra escape back into the kjarr.

"Come with me," he said. "I'll introduce you to everyone."

There were no enemies at the Blue-eyed Festival. While this was a promise every guest made by attending, there was something more to it. Even gryphons and opinici who had found themselves on opposite sides of the conflict had reached some sort of personal understanding. While the village of Crane's Nest had dedicated itself to stopping Satra, Tresh had only been able to save her brother's mate with the Ashen Weald's help. Satra and Tresh chatted happily about Quess's recovery.

When Satra and Zeph interacted, the questions they had for each other remained unasked. Past criticisms were forgotten. Younce had let Zeph and the others know about his plans, and they did their best to make Satra feel welcome.

Once the Kjarr had met all of the taiga gryphons and guests, Younce gathered everyone who had known Mignet. They headed down into the caverns. He nodded to Tresh. She'd promised to act as host in his absence.

TO SATRA'S SURPRISE, the cavern was warm and well-lit. Braziers lined the surrounding walls, which were full of paintings of past events. While several Blue-eyed Festivals were recorded here, so was the Connixation. There was a drawing of Williwaw with graves around it. Another of Hoarfrost, a frozen catacomb until it had been reopened last autumn.

Eleven pride glyphs were blackened with charcoal to show they no longer existed. Satra had never seen ten of the pride glyphs before. The gravestone next to Williwaw had been modified, and a frozen island painted next to it recently. Williwaw lived on, even if they weren't willing to come back to the mainland that had killed most of their kin.

She'd walked this path to the springs once before, long ago. There'd been no light then, but Mignet's blue eyes let her see this far down. Satra had been terrified. On her own, she'd never have considered sneaking into another pride's nesting grounds, let alone into a cave. Only Mignet's guidance had allowed her to find her way into the hot water. They'd had hours alone, the best of Satra's life, up until...

"Do you remember when Younce and I came down here and caught you and Mignet?" Zeph asked.

Satra wasn't sure what to say. She felt like she'd been caught all over again.

"I always wondered how you got home," Younce said. "You were soaked through and through."

Thenca laughed. "Deracho, that's how."

They looked at the owl gryphon, who was finally awake. "I'll let Satra tell it, if she wants it told."

Now Satra had everyone looking at her. "There's really not much to tell. Zeph and Younce nearly scared us out of our fur. We fled upstairs before Mignet's father caught us. I ran into Deracho near the entrance, and he let me hide in his den while Mignet kept her father distracted. Deracho escorted me home in the morning, once I was dry."

"What did your pride do when they found out?" Younce asked.

"They never did," Thenca said. "I told them that because of Satra's poor hunting skills, I'd forced her to stay out all night hunting swamp grouse."

"And you told *me* that if I ever did that again, you'd feed me to the turtles," Satra laughed. "I'm grateful, though. I don't know what the den mother would have done otherwise."

Thenca snorted. "Well, I *like* you, but I *love* Deracho, and he suggested the night hunting ruse."

Deracho slow blinked at Satra. "You two weren't the only set of kjarr and taiga gryphons who met when their hunting territories butted up against each other."

Satra felt a pang of guilt. After Mignet's death, the split between the taiga and kjarr pride had kept Thenca and Deracho apart for years. She was about to apologize when Younce spoke up. While she'd assumed this would all be about her, she was surprised to hear his story.

"So nobody loved sugar frogs as much as Mignet, right?" Younce asked. "She had a bit of a sweet beak."

Zeph and Deracho nodded, but Satra didn't. She didn't know this about Mignet. They'd mostly eaten whatever they happened to catch while hunting, usually frost chickens.

"One day," Younce continued, "when Deracho was out training Zeph to hunt, Mignet and I came up with a plan."

Zeph and Deracho looked at each other, unsure where this was going.

Younce continued. "It was mostly Mignet's plan. I can say that because she's not here to tell you otherwise. See, she heard from Satra that every time Deracho secretly met with Thenca, he brought her a sugar frog. So Mignet thought that Deracho *must* have a secret frog stash hidden somewhere."

"It's true," Thenca confirmed. "Mignet wasn't the only one with a sweet beak. I had to finally cut back because I'd put on so many pounds that people could tell me and Urious apart. There's nothing like having a thin twin brother to force you to reconsider your eating habits."

"You could've had Deracho bring two frogs," Satra suggested. "One for you and one for Urious."

"Well, I didn't actually tell my brother I was seeing a taiga gryphon," Thenca admitted. "He'd fallen hard for Ari, but she wouldn't pay him any mind. He was so morose; I didn't want him to know I was sneaking off at night."

Satra laughed, but she was also surprised. Thenca and Urious had taken care of her when she was younger. They'd provided a unified front, so she'd assumed they did everything together. She'd never considered the internal politics of having a lookalike.

"Anyways," Younce continued, "we searched his nest while he was off with Thenca but didn't have any luck."

"You searched his cave?" Zeph laughed. "For a frozen frog? It would have defrosted."

"Hey, you weren't any smarter as a gryphlet," Younce countered. "We eventually realized that for the frog to still be frozen by the time he reached the kjarr grounds, he must be hiding them somewhere along the way."

Satra's heart leapt. She was afraid he'd say the frogs had been hidden at the pond where Mignet had drowned.

"We searched everywhere," he continued, "but eventually the only place we could think of was the waterfall. The one that forms the river that goes right into the kjarr."

"Oh no," Deracho said.

"Oh yes," Younce replied. "We found Deracho's hidden stash. I only had room for one or two frogs, but Mignet, she wanted them all."

Sugar frogs were almost sickly-sweet. When the taiga froze, the frogs froze with it. In the spring, they'd defrost and go back to being frogs. But something about the way they froze turned them incredibly sweet. Eating two was already a good way to get an upset stomach.

"While I nursed my stomach ache," Younce continued, "she kept digging. See, Deracho had frozen nearly a hundred frogs!"

"Well, that does explain how you always had one," Thenca said. "I did wonder where you were getting all the frogs from."

Deracho's nares blushed. "The waterfall was high enough that it was still frigid up there long after the aneda forests began to thaw. I spent all autumn catching frogs and bringing them to the waterfall to freeze for later."

"What happened?" Satra asked. "Mignet didn't really eat a hundred frogs, did she?"

"Well, she wanted to," Younce said, "but she didn't actually get to eat any of them. She was so busy digging up the frozen frogs and putting them in a pile, she didn't realize they were defrosting. It took her over an hour, but she dug up all hundred of those frogs. Except when she put the hundredth on the pile, the first twenty were hopping away."

Deracho shook his head. Satra couldn't blame him. An autumn's hard work, gone in an hour.

"She started chasing the frogs, trying to get them back into the pile. By the time she'd finally gathered the frogs, they'd all defrosted." Younce paused to laugh. "Poor Mignet! The *frogs* were hopping everywhere, and *she* was hopping mad. She tried to grab one and hold it under the waterfall, but it didn't refreeze and turn sweet. She managed to steal all of Deracho's frogs, but she didn't manage to eat any of them."

"Serves her right!" Deracho said.

Thenca was laughing and couldn't stop. "It does explain why I stopped getting sweet treats so often. I wish I could have seen the expression on Deracho's face."

Younce had a mischievous grin on his face. "By that

time, we knew Deracho would be back with Zeph at any moment, so we high-tailed it out of there."

"What did you think happened?" Zeph asked Deracho. "You didn't think the frogs had dug themselves out, did you?"

"I considered it," Deracho admitted. "Sometimes goliath birds reach unusual heights. I assumed one must have spent all day digging up my frogs. I had no idea the 'goliath birds' were part of my own pride!"

The stories continued into the night, until a mishap with the cooking braziers sent everyone except Younce and Satra up top to sort it out.

YOUNCE KNEW he should probably head up top to help, but Tresh was capable and had promised to keep track of things until Satra was okay.

"How are you?" he asked Satra. "It's not too much, is it?"

"A bit." Her posture was stiff. "The Mignet you grew up with and the Mignet I knew in the hunting grounds almost feel like two different gryphons. Except for the hot springs, I don't think I ever saw who she was around her friends and family. And none of you ever saw who she was around me. It doesn't feel like we're remembering the same gryphon."

"We're all a little different around those we care about," Younce admitted. "There's a mountain nearby where Mignet and I used to visit a different hot spring. Not like you and her visited this one, mind you, but the steam kept us warm as we looked up at the stars and talked.

"Most of what Mignet chatted about was you. There's something stifling about the taiga pride. I've done my best to change things, but the feeling is still there. We have one nesting grounds, and we don't leave it often. Heading down to the shore is hot and humid, neither of which are pleasant with a thick coat. But for those *without* a thick coat, Snowfall is too cold to visit. And with so few taiga gryphons, there're no opportunities to find love here. It's like being stuck in a cave with your siblings all year long."

Satra dipped a paw into the hot springs.

"Mignet used to talk about you all the time. To Zeph, to me, to anyone she could trust to keep her secret," he continued. "We were all jealous. It seemed unlikely we'd meet anyone we didn't already know. And when Zeph fledged and his feathers stayed brown, we knew he wouldn't be staying with us. We'd be losing a friend."

"Instead, you lost two friends," Satra said.

Younce didn't acknowledge her comment. He could hear the sounds of the others returning. "Mignet found someone who made her happy, and that was you. You may not know what she was like growing up, you may not have heard what she was like around her other friends, but we heard about what she was like around you because that was important to her. You made her happy."

"I also made her dead." There was a brittle edge to Satra's voice.

"Gryphons die all the time." This wasn't where Younce thought he was going to take this, but since they were here, he went all in. "Right after fledging is when we're most likely to die. The air currents, the goliath birds, the ice—as painful as it is to admit, as much as I hope to change things, that's the life we lead."

He considered his next words. "We're all mad that Mignet is dead. We're not mad that you were with her when she drowned. The only gryphon who blamed you—her father—was wrong to do so. He didn't know how much you meant to her."

By now, the others had returned and heard the echoes of conversation as they descended to the springs.

Deracho came back in first. "If he'd been any sort of leader, he'd have invited you here the first Blue-eyed Festival after her death to mourn for her."

"If we'd been better friends to Mignet," Zeph continued, "we'd have gone into the kjarr that first year and brought the Blue-eyed Festival to you."

"But we didn't," Younce said. "That was our mistake. And then Zeph was sent away."

"And the war between the kjarr and Crackling Sea happened," Thenca added.

"Right," Younce continued, "and you never got a chance to know that it wasn't your fault, that no one blames you, and..."

Here he hesitated. He didn't know if it was too soon or not, but it was the real reason he'd invited Satra here. While he knew gryphons never tended to form long-term romantic bonds, the shaking up of the status quo had allowed some gryphons to act more like opinici. As unlikely as it was that his own relationship with Tresh would continue when the mating season ended—she'd freeze up here, he'd melt at Swan's Rest—he had begun to understand the desire to be with just one gryphon and to have that relationship acknowledged.

But there was something else Younce wanted Satra to know. "It's okay to move on. Everyone here, everyone who knew and loved Mignet, we know that you loved her, too. The fact that she loved you and she's dead can be a burden. But all of us are here if you need a friend, and all of us will still be here if you find someone else."

Satra's posture was rigid, and her ears were flat. Finally, either from force of will or the heat of the springs, she softened and said, "Thank you. Honestly, thank all of you."

Younce slow blinked in the friendly manner of a gryphon. "So much talking. You've got to be tired of sitting on the edges of the hot springs. Let's get wet!"

Zeph was about to make his escape back up the cavern when Younce pounced him into the water with a splash that soaked the walls of the room.

Thenca was right behind him, pushing Deracho into the water. Taiga fur took forever to dry. After all of the trauma Satra had been through, no one pushed her, but she slipped in of her own accord and joined the splashing.

Between the talking, swimming, and heat, it wasn't long before they were all starving. With a bit of help, everyone got the taiga gryphons dry enough to go back into the amphitheater, and they ascended to the celebration.

Satra stared out at the snowstorm, which hadn't let up since she arrived. She wanted to get a better look, but her undercoat was still damp, and she was afraid to stray from the heat of the brazier. All around her, gryphons and opinici were celebrating and chatting. Zeph returned to Kia's side. Thenca and Deracho disappeared back to his cave. Satra even heard a snort that sounded suspiciously like her off-work bodyguard, Foultner, chatting with an ex-Reeve's Guard.

Only Younce's islanders hadn't accepted the invitation. She understood the feeling. There were days where she felt a deep sense of loyalty to the Ashen Weald and the next generation of kjarr gryphons, but there were also days when she'd love to disappear to an island for a year to sort out her thoughts.

She looked over at Younce, who was spending time with Tresh. She caught his eye, his bright blue eye, and he grabbed a sugar frog and came over to drop it at her feet.

"No sign of your islanders," Satra said. "With the snowstorm, I don't know if you should take that personally."

"I know!" He sighed. "And here I'd heard the Williwaw Pride were the best flyers, better than even fantails. Just think, the gryphons who were brave enough to fly through the Connixation were too scared to come to my party."

"Do they have feathered tails?" she asked.

"That's what the fisherfolk say." He looked out at the snowstorm with her.

"Like Mignet," she said.

"Like Mignet," he confirmed. "Her father was a Snowfall gryphon through and through, but I sometimes wondered about her mother's side. Was it the opinicus? Or was she descended from a Williwaw gryphon?"

"Hmmm." In the hours Satra had spent talking to Mignet, it had sounded like what she wanted most in the world was to see the Crackling Sea Eyrie. She'd hatched there, but as soon as her mother saw she was a gryphon, she'd brought Mignet to live with her father in the mountains. More than anything, Mignet had wanted to see the beautiful electric sea and spend time with her mother.

Satra had been to the Crackling Sea, both as a prisoner and a conqueror. She'd fished through the bloody sands to find the wingfeathers of the gryphons she loved. She'd seen the sea explode with lightning. She'd fought the monsters in its depths—and its heights, if she counted the opinici who roosted there.

When she'd stood with an army at her back and taken

the eyrie, she heard her father's voice telling her to scourge all life, to turn the eyrie into a tomb the same way the Connixation had done to Hoarfrost. But when the storm-cloth curtains fell, Satra had seen the eyrie through Mignet's eyes.

Mignet had died before the wars, before the wingtorn, before the weald burned to ash and the eyries fell. Satra appreciated what Younce and his friends were trying to do by giving her permission to move past Mignet. At the same time, Satra wasn't ready. She needed her connection to Mignet to keep her from doing the wrong thing. As the past years had proven, the wrong thing was often easier.

Someday, Satra would find someone new, but not tonight. Not while she ruled so many. Mignet's love and optimism were frozen in time. They had survived the war where Satra's hadn't, and she'd lean on them until she no longer had to rule.

The snowstorm worsened, turning the sky more white than black. The braziers flickered as wind shifted under the stormcloth roof. When the white faded, patches of snow seemed to hang in the air.

Not snow, she thought. *Gryphons.*

"They're beautiful," Satra said.

Twenty gryphons caught the high winds and froze in the air, their long wings and streamer-like tails catching the current. When the winds died down, they began to glide towards the brazier light.

The Williwaw Pride had returned home.

SNOW & LIGHT

AUTHOR'S NOTE

You made it! You survived losing Mignet. You survived the Connixation. You survived a mountain of infected snowy owl gryphons. You even survived the guests at your Blue-eyed Festival. And now you've made it to the author's note.

First, let's talk a little about the inspiration for the stories. Later, we'll get to my confession.

Satra and Mignet was a story I've had in mind for a long time. I wanted an opportunity to show the characters happy, which is why I stopped right as the ice cracked. It's not an exaggeration to say that my mailing list quadrupled in size the moment I offered a *lesbian beak-cute gryphon love story with terror birds* as the free short story for a while. I wanted to give readers an opportunity to love Mignet as much as Satra did. I hope I succeeded there.

I never planned to write about the Connixation, but how could I not in a short story collection about taiga gryphons? Several novels ago, we had our first hints of taiga fisherfolk living far off the coast. Yet I planned to write a happy story from the taiga prides at the height of their power. In *Starling,*

I wrote about Younce trying to send messages to those islanders, and yet I planned to write a story set right before the Connixation without touching on them.

Well, that didn't work out. What started as a hoppy, happy story quickly devolved into the line, "This is how the world ends." Gryphon versus nature, the fourth type of literary conflict. I hope getting a glimpse into the apocalypse wasn't too gloomy.

If "Blue Eyes" was a new love story, "Silver Eyes" is an old relationship tale. Deracho and Thenca were on the cover of *Ashen Weald* together, but we never got to see inside his fuzzy little brain until now. I didn't include Younce or Zeph there with him this time because poor Deracho deserved a break. I've had a few fans write in asking how the Ashen Weald's gryphon-opinicus culture combination was affecting both sides. This story is my answer to that question.

"Blue-eyed Festival" was actually the first story I wrote and the last I edited. Like Younce, I think it's hard to comfort our friends who have lost romantic partners. I never know what to do or say, even if my heart goes out to them. Instead, I gave Satra room to grieve—or not, as she thought best.

Next up, *Reevesbane* will take place as the world begins to thaw. It's time to bring Zeph and Kia back to the weald just in time for the Blackwing Eyrie's forces to show up at their doorstep.

And now for my wintertime confession: I don't remember much of the winter. The same catastrophic APS event that nearly killed me and caused multiple organ failure wiped out large parts of my memory like a magnet over an old hard drive. My descriptions of the cold of the Connixation are really my memories of getting dialysis in the middle of a blizzard. There's a kind of cold that never leaves you, the cold of having your blood taken and returned on a day where the thermometer has gone into the negatives.

What's more, with my memories gone, I only have stories from other people about past holiday events— making snow cats in Virginia, juggling snowballs, Christmas bats, eggnog, all of it. They're stories my loved ones tell about a character who shares my name but who isn't me because I no longer have those memories.

I can't do anything about that. Unlike television, the memories aren't hiding somewhere waiting for the right phrase to unlock again. I have a scan showing where the clot damage happened—a white spot of winter snow on my brain. Instead, I have stories that ring false no matter how much I trust the teller.

The best I can do is try to make new memories. Part of that is writing about the taiga pride in winter. Who doesn't want to see a snowstorm and think of Tielle flying ahead of a wall of clouds, leading her pride to safety? I'd rather have that than memories of dialysis. But I'm also planning to try to make new memories of the ice and snow.

Well, I say ice and snow: I mean Florida. Where I grew up, Christmas Eve is spent on the beach filling luminaires with sand and candles and then lining the roads with them. (In Colorado, we'd call that a fire hazard. In Florida, it's just as likely to get rained out.) My mom has lived in the same home by the beach for forty years, but she's finally ready to move on, and she's invited everyone home to have one last Christmas in the old house.

What stories do you tell of the holidays? Feel free to

reach out and let me know. Without my own memories to rely upon, the best I can do is hear everyone else's.

Blue Eyes and Other Tales is a small rest stop halfway through the series. We're gearing up towards the last stretch, full of —well, spoilers. It's best to leave it as a surprise.

I've loved working on this series. I started this journey in 2017 with Zeph stuck halfway up a tree, ready to pounce on some parrots. I've delighted in every new gryphon and opinicus. Honestly, I've never had more fun writing anything than I've enjoyed writing gryphons. The moment you finish reading this Author's Note, you should go write your own gryphon books. Then you'll see just how fun it can be.

It's been a strange journey thus far, and I mean that in a good way. I held the first copies of *Eyrie* in my hand. I signed and sent out five hardcovers, ten, twenty, thirty, a hundred. I watched as two more books were released. I met other gryphon fans—and some of you have gryphon shelves to rival my own! I connected with the authors of the gryphon books I was reading in my free time. I even helped a few new gryphon authors get their books published. Meanwhile, as a new author myself, I was invited out to spend a week with Mercedes Lackey and Larry Dixon, the legends who wrote the gryphon stories of my childhood.

A lot happened I never would have expected. A lot happened that never would have had I not first wrote about a small gryphon hunting rather large ground parrots. I'm in awe of the last few years.

Don't worry, though, we still have a lot of novels left together. And, if you're willing to try out some fantasy set in worlds without gryphons, even more to come. I'm grateful for the time we've had together. I look forward to seeing you again at the end of *Reevesbane*.

Until then, may your winters be full of snow and light, stories and good food, love and friendship.

-Vale

K. VALE NAGLE

EYRIE
GRYPHON INSURRECTION: BOOK ONE

K. VALE NAGLE

ASHEN
WEALD
GRYPHON INSURRECTION: BOOK TWO

K. VALE NAGLE

STARLING
GRYPHON INSURRECTION: BOOK THREE

K. VALE NAGLE

REEVESBANE
GRYPHON INSURRECTION: BOOK FOUR

K. VALE NAGLE

THE RUINS OF
CRESTFALL
GRYPHON INSURRECTION: BOOK FIVE

K. VALE NAGLE

OPINICUS
GRYPHON INSURRECTION: BOOK SIX

ABOUT THE AUTHOR

K. Vale Nagle is alarmingly hard to kill. While he's written his entire life, after surviving a pulmonary embolism and multiple organ failure, he began to take his writing more seriously and worked to get a degree in creative writing while recovering.

During that time another embolism struck and failed to kill him, at which point the doctors discovered an undiagnosed autoimmune disorder and patched him back up. Having used up two of his nine lives, he began publishing short stories and novels. When the doctors said that lung surgery was a 95% certainty, he dyed his hair dark blue, which is when he discovered that he was so unwell that his hair wasn't growing. A year later, and a switch from dark blue to teal, and his hair has finally started growing again (albeit silver instead of its pre-embolism black) and he's writing like a fiend.

Now, Vale writes feral fantasy—books with mythological creatures and nature-based settings, often involving gryphons and conflict.

He can be found online at kvalenagle.com, via his news-letter, or on Patreon at Patreon.com/kvalenagle.

facebook.com/kvalenagle

twitter.com/kvalenagle

bookbub.com/authors/k-vale-nagle

ALSO BY K. VALE NAGLE

www.ingramcontent.com/pod-product-compliance
Lightning Source LLC
Chambersburg PA
CBHW020722130726
47899CB00011B/970